BOOKS BY DANIEL BREEZE
Brains
We're Having a Heat Wave

WE'RE HAVING A HEAT WAVE

Daniel Breeze

McNeil & Richards

| ISBN 13 | 978-0-9825602-5-9 |
| ISBN | 0-9825602-5-7 |

Published by McNeil & Richards
USA

For Gayla

Contents

I

CHILI & LIGHTNING

1

Handling the weather at our little television station, WWTT in Toledo, Ohio, is a little like shooting yourself in the foot every night at 6 P.M. and 11 P.M. There's no sane reason for doing it. In my case, I accepted the job because no one else would hire me as a weatherman. It was WWTT or unemployment.

There are days when I think I made the wrong choice.

At the time I am writing about, I had been the WWTT weatherman for three years. Over that span, I had learned a few things about the weather and a great deal about how management can drive a business into the ground. Pauley Sherman, our station manager, and Bengobar, the corporation that owned our little station, had proven very skillful in that aspect of business.

Pauley and I have what would be called—in more luxurious surroundings—"creative differences" about how the weather should be presented. I believe extensive weather coverage should dominate the local news. Pauley believes weathermen should act like clowns to bring in the crowds, then get out of the way so advertisers can sell their wares to them. Obviously there is a huge gap between our viewpoints, and just as obviously I am right. (Let Pauley write his own book.)

The momentous events that changed both our lives began on a cool December evening when Pauley—a thirty-two-year-old wunderkind who had been hired six months earlier to turn things around at WWTT—slithered into my weather cubbyhole as I was tracking storms on my computer. Incidentally, I was four years younger than Pauley and much better looking.

"A word of advice," he said. "Don't chow down at lunch tomorrow. Save room for a bowl of free chili."

I knew what was coming. I tried to head Pauley off before he bushwhacked me. "Forget it, Pauley. I'm not doing any more remotes from chili suppers, fish fries, county fairs, or your grandmother's house."

He ignored me. "It's all set. Tuesday evening, you'll do a remote from a charity chili supper in Ottawa Hills. Eric will drive the van over and handle the camerawork."

I explained to Pauley for the umpteenth time that it was beneath the dignity of a weatherman to mess around at chili suppers and pancake breakfasts. Pauley disagreed.

"Willard Scott once delivered the weather for the 'Today' show dressed as Carmen Miranda," he pointed out.

"Some weathermen do it," I conceded, "but the National Meteorological Society frowns on that sort of thing."

"You aren't a member of the N.M.S.," Pauley noted.

"That's right. And do you know why? They won't let me in because you force me to do remotes from chili suppers and fish frys. Wouldn't you like to have a meteorologist who's recognized by a national organization deliver the weather for you?"

"Then who would I send to the chili suppers and fish frys?"

"Nobody!" I said. "It's not worth it!"

"We've had this discussion before, Sheldon. You can fly off to cover hurricanes, tornadoes and plugged-up bathroom drains on your own time, but what you get paid for is reading the weather forecast and showing up at the chili suppers. The Nielsens show our ratings go up when you do remotes! Look, if it would get higher ratings, I'd have you do the weather from the Kitty Kat Klub in your birthday suit."

Pauley worried me. With an attitude like that, he was network material.

"What I'm telling you, Sheldon, is that if you can't do things my way, I'm sure I could find a weatherman who will."

TUESDAY, DECEMBER 2

As I drove to Ottawa Hills the next afternoon for the chili supper, light rain splattered the windshield of my Buick Skylark. I had assured viewers it would not rain on Tuesday, but it was doing it just the same.

Ottawa Hills is a village of about 4,500 people on the west side of Toledo. (If you have ever been stranded in Toledo, you know that it's a city of about 290,000 in northwest Ohio on the western end of Lake Erie. If you cross the city limits on the north, you're in Michigan.)

As I drove, I was in a bad mood not only because of the rain but because I was frustrated by Pauley's Weatherman-As-Clown philosophy. My career hung in the balance because I balked at making a fool of myself at chili suppers and charity barbecues. A hero of mine—David Ludlum, one of the first television weathermen in Philadelphia—had been fired because he refused to croon a weather ditty. He later wrote several books on the weather and founded *Weatherwise* magazine. But if I were fired for refusing to do a chili supper remote, my future was likely to be less rosy. It was quite possible no other station would hire me, and I had no idea what I would do if I were not a weatherman.

Being a weatherman was all I had ever wanted to do, and I threw myself into it enthusiastically. I could never be the kind of weather jockey who cracked a few jokes, cooked up fancy graphics and served up the same forecast any jerk could get by dialing the National Weather Service. I wanted to be out where the weather was happening. I wanted to be on the frontlines, not down in the shelters. Two months earlier, when devastating Hurricane Helga bore down on Florida, I flew to Miami to confront the hurricane. After Miami broadcasters headed for the shelters, I was still on the air, telling people back in Toledo about the hurricane. Miami was crumbling around me, but I was on the air!

Okay, so that wasn't one of my sanest moments. I did it for three reasons: I wanted to be where the action was, I wanted to tell people back in Toledo what was happening, and in the back of my mind was the notion that a Miami television station might hire me as their weatherman. They didn't go for the bait.

My point is this: going the extra mile—such as reporting from the middle of disasters—can help people. And so can accurate forecasts, by warning about approaching storms, and so can long-range forecasts, by saving businesses and farmers millions of dollars.

That's the kind of forecasting I wanted to do, but explaining it to Pauley Sherman was like trying to sell girlie magazines to the Pope. Give me some bucks, I told Pauley, and I can tell you if it's going to rain at three in the afternoon four months from now. Pauley's answer was (1) the station didn't have the bucks, and (2) he didn't care whether it would rain at three in the afternoon four months from now. According to Pauley's theory of television station management, cheaper was always better.

Old Harley Carruthers, one of the instructors at the Toledo Weather College, had warned me that weather forecasting was a tough business. "You must learn about isobars, altocumulous clouds, squaw lines and ass kissing," he asserted. I couldn't figure out what squaw lines had to do with the weather. I thought that was what they called country line dancing when Indian women did it. Old Harley growled, "not squaws, you moron! Squalls!"

Nevertheless, I understood the point old Harley was making about ass kissing. I thought I would be able to stay above all that and wouldn't need to dirty my hands with station politics, but I was wrong. There are always Pauley Shermans who can fire you if you don't do things *their* way.

As I neared Ottawa Hills, the temperature hovered around 42 degrees and rain was still falling. I braced myself, because I knew that half of the people at the chili supper would blame me for the crummy weather. They forget that weathermen don't manufacture the weather, we merely forecast it. The other half would ridicule me for blowing the forecast.

"You blew it today, didn't you, Jer!"

I had never met the old geezer in the beret before he approached me at the chili supper, but when people see you night after night on television, they feel they know you.

"I sure did. I spend so many hours at chili suppers and charity rummage sales I don't have time to figure out what the weather's going to be."

He nodded knowingly. "I figured it was somethin' like that."

He wandered off in the general direction of the chili pots.

I glanced around the cavernous hall where three hundred or so people were chowing down and realized that in the distance Dexter Bentley and a crew from WORY were setting up to do a remote. I winced at the thought of having to put up with that buffoon and his jibes about "the kid forecaster at that other station". Dexter not only enjoyed doing remotes from chili suppers, he begged his boss to set them up. We're not talking about weather forecaster integrity here. We're talking about raw, unabashed showboating.

Eric Larkin, a young sandy-haired cameraman, arrived in one of the two WWTT remote vans five minutes after I did.

"Let's set up over here," I told him. "It's about as far from Dexter as I can get without leaving the building."

One of the ladies in charge of the occasion approached and insisted I sample the chili. I didn't want to taste the damn chili so I politely refused. She persisted.

"Come on, Jerry. You really must taste the chili. It's heavenly!"

"I can't right now," I said. "We're setting up for our remote, and I don't have time—"

She shoved a spoonful of chili in front of my mouth. "It will just take a moment. Please taste it!"

I took a mouthful. Immediately my throat burned like Hades. My eyes opened wide. I thought my brains were going to explode. No one told me it was red hot chili, the kind Texans use to pave roads when they run out of tar.

"Water!" I managed to gasp. "I need water!"

I swear I didn't know Dexter had come up behind me. When he tapped on my shoulder, I turned around and was so surprised to see him standing close to me that I opened my mouth and sprayed him with chili.

He seemed shocked and bewildered.

"What the hell did you do that for, kid?"

He had heard my name hundreds of time when he monitored our weathercasts. He just didn't want to remember it.

"I'm sorry, old man. I didn't know you were behind me." I gulped down the glass of water a kind soul had fetched. Then I started wiping chili off the apron Dexter had donned for the occasion. He pushed my hands away because he thought I was making it worse by smearing the chili into the fabric. And I was.

"I'll take care of it. I can't believe this! I go on the air in ten minutes and you splattered me with chili!"

I suppose I should have felt sorry for Dexter, but this was the same weatherman who once shot a duck out of the sky to prove it was a clear day, just as he had predicted.

"You're a menace," Dexter grumbled. "Why don't you go back to Florida. Maybe the next hurricane will blow your head off. . . . What were you doing down there anyway?"

"Every once in a while I like to be where the action is, Dexter. It reminds me there's more to the weather than chili suppers and fish frys. You ought to try it some time."

He shook his head. "All a TV weatherman needs to do is get the crowd into the tent. Then you give them the forecast, and everything else is frosting on the cake. Don't make a big deal out of it. All the fancy equipment you can buy won't give you a better forecast."

"Uh-huh. What are you using over at your station to forecast the weather this week—pig spleens or aching joints? Or maybe the old adage 'when the cow scratches its ear, it means a shower is near'."

"Let's face it, kid. You didn't predict the rain tonight, the Weather Service didn't, and I didn't. You may feel like you're better than the rest of us, but your forecasts ain't any better."

He hurried away in a huff, still wiping chili off his apron.

"Stand by," ordered Barb Farley, the director back at the station. I heard her voice in my earpiece.

"How am I getting paid this week?" I asked. "In dollars—or chili beans?"

"Don't even joke about that," Barb said. "If Pauley thought he could get away with it, he *would* pay us in chili beans. . . .Three ... two ... one . . ."

I launched into my opening:

"WE'RE HERE IN OTTAWA HILLS AT THE JUNIOR BASKETBALL LEAGUE BENEFIT CHILI SUPPER, AND I BET YOU WISH YOU WERE HERE, FOLKS. MANY CELEBRITIES ARE IN THE CROWD. THE FIRE CHIEF IS OVER IN THE CORNER, OUT IN THE HALLWAY A BOY ACQUITTED OF MURDER IS BEATING UP HIS LITTLE BROTHER, AND ON THE FAR SIDE OF THE ROOM DEXTER BENTLEY IS MOPPING CHILI OFF HIS CLOTHES. SOME PEOPLE CAN'T HOLD THEIR CHILI. ... WELL, LET'S GET RIGHT INTO TODAY'S WEATHER STATISTICS. THE HIGH IN TOLEDO WAS 45 . . ."

2

When I left the chili supper, I was still upset because my dignity as a weatherman had been compromised by yet another frivolous remote broadcast, and my mood was further dampened because not only had I failed to forecast the rain showers earlier in the evening, I had completely missed the thunderstorms that followed. Rain poured out of the heavens like booze on the day before Prohibition. Crashing thunder accompanied flashes of lightning. I was in one of those "I don't need this kind of aggravation!" moods most of us get into at one time or another. I contemplated getting drunk, quitting my job, or leaving town—or perhaps all three.

By the time I arrived at the WWTT offices to prepare for the 11 P.M. newscast, I was drenched.

Toledo supports a slew of AM and FM radio stations and five television stations. WWTT is the smallest of the television stations. Our offices are housed in a two-story concrete building north of downtown Toledo on Alexis Road. The news operation is tucked away on the second floor.

As I hurried into the newsroom, co-anchor Brent Lassiter

commented, "Looks like some of those partly cloudy skies fell on you."

Brent had been hired twenty years earlier because he looked like an anchor should look—handsome, square-jawed, authoritative, friendly. He still considered himself handsome, but over the years his teeth had rotted, his hair had thinned out, and he had gained twenty pounds. The station didn't get rid of Brent because he was a Toledo institution. He was like a familiar old sofa that's falling apart. The owner hesitates to throw it away because it has sentimental value. Brent was WWTT's old sofa.

Fran Rosen, his streetwise co-anchor, remarked, "those chili suppers must be worse than I remember."

"They're brutal," I grumbled.

Fran, thirtyish and attractive, was a victim of the "Catch 22" of the broadcasting business: you can't get a better job without job experience, but if you work for WWTT nobody else wants to hire you.

Morty Greer told me, "I've seen guys who played in the Super Bowl come out lookin' better than you."

Morty was our forty-three-year-old sports anchor. Six-foot-four and lean, he looked as though he could still play semi-pro basketball. Morty floated through life in a stupor. He loved Toledo, he adored his job, and he was crazy about all of Toledo's sports teams. He didn't know who was president, and he couldn't figure out what kept space shuttles from falling out of the sky, but he could tell you that George Mikan averaged 28.3 points per game playing for Minneapolis in 1949.

I was ticked off by my colleagues' remarks and I'm afraid I took it out on Morty. "Why don't you cover the basketball games and shuffleboard tournaments and stop buttin' in where you don't belong?" I grumbled.

Morty looked as though he had been slapped. As I stomped off to the weather cubbyhole, Morty asked, "What's the matter with him?"

"Jerry blew the forecast again," Brent said.

In my cubbyhole, I slipped off my dripping wet sport coat and draped it over a bust of Thomas Jefferson. I kept Jefferson around because he had been something of a weatherman himself, recording detailed observations about atmospheric conditions.

Anxious to put the annoyances of the evening behind me, I fired up the Cloudchaser computer and browsed through the latest National Weather Service data. Raw data and weather charts would enable me to create sophisticated weather graphics that would clearly illustrate where the storm fronts were. Thanks to animation, I could give viewers a "fly-over" showing how cloud formations and weather conditions would look if you were flying above them. It was a far cry from the hand-drawn maps and stick-on symbols employed by television weathercasters in the '40s and '50s.

As I worked, I was only faintly aware of the thunder outside, and I had completely forgotten the manufacturer's warning about exercising caution when using the computer during lightning storms. I was on deadline and had no time to worry about such details.

I recall mumbling something about the incompetence of Dexter Bentley and wondering aloud why God had humiliated me by opening the spigots of heaven when I hadn't forecast it. Then I launched into a one-sided conversation with Him.

"The weather is a mess!" I grumbled. "I'm tired of getting all the blame for it and having none of the responsibility, none of the control. . . . You've got a lot of other things to do—let *me* handle the weather!"

I was plotting the path of a low pressure area through the Southwest when suddenly an incredibly bright light flashed across the computer monitor. Electricity flowed from the keyboard into my body. My fingertips smoked, my hair frizzled, and my eyes opened wide. The same thing had happened the last time I tasted my fianceé's lasagna, but this time Laura's cooking was not to blame. Lightning had struck the power lines, power surged into the computer, and then it surged into me!

The newsroom crew heard my outcry—Fran later described it as the "wail of a wounded moose"—and someone had the presence of mind to pick up a phone and dial 411.

That's right. They didn't dial 911, the emergency number, they called local information. Thus, the ambulance was delayed an extra four minutes in arriving at the station and my brain baked four minutes longer than would otherwise have been necessary.

3

Because my mind had been temporarily short-circuited, my memories of the ensuing few hours are rather disconnected and downright weird. I vaguely recall the ambulance driver complaining that I had sustained such an electrical charge I was interfering with his radio transmission. I mumbled an apology. When ambulance attendants carted me into the emergency room at St. Vincent Medical Center, television sets went haywire. The nurse who took my pulse complained that I had given her an electrical shock.

As a doctor gave me a handful of painkillers to swallow, he suggested I was lucky. "It could have been a lot worse. Lightning kills about a hundred Americans each year."

I wondered how many of them had been under his care. He then proceeded to relate an amusing little anecdote about a bolt of lightning that hit a home in 1977, melting the refrigerator and cooking a five-pound ham. (When I received his bill two or three weeks later, I noted he had charged me $185 for relating that bit of information.)

After examining me off and on for about two hours, he concluded I had a few burns on my body and my fingers were unusually red. A brain scan revealed nothing, but an impromptu experiment showed that when I touched a television set, it could receive thirty-five channels without being hooked up to cable.

As I waited in the ER to be admitted to the hospital for an overnight stay, I listened to the late-evening WWTT news. Brent Lassiter reported I would not be delivering the weather because I had been incapacitated by a lightning-induced power surge. Fran suggested that was impossible . . . there couldn't have been any lightning because I hadn't forecast it. Then Brent, Fran and Morty Greer all had a good laugh. Our newsroom crew had never been very good at engaging in Happy Talk.

Laura Matthews, my fianceé, came to visit me and I remained in the hospital overnight.

Laura was a shapely twenty-nine-year-old brunette divorcee who worked at Dillard's department store in the Westfield Franklin Park shopping mall. I had met her two years earlier. We had not set a date for our wedding. Although she had agreed to marry me in one of her weaker moments, when the moon was high, the fire was low and the wine was flowing, we had never agreed on when we would tie the knot. I had the definite feeling she wasn't sure she wanted to marry me. She reminded me of the magazine *Scientific American*, which for years published on its cover an illustration of a clock showing how close mankind was to nuclear war. Some years, the clock indicated we were within two or three "minutes" of Doomsday. Other years, when the international climate was less heated, the clock was set to maybe ten or fifteen minutes before twelve. Well, Laura had a clock of her own, a marriage clock. Some months, we were within two or three minutes of Doomsday—I mean, our Wedding Day—and other months, we were several hours away from Doomsday. It all depended on how she felt about me at the time.

"What did you do this time?" she asked, implying that the power surge was somehow my fault.

I didn't feel like going into details. "I don't have any idea."

"Well, don't do it again."

"I don't plan on it."

Other men, they wind up in the hospital, their women burst into tears. "Oh, darling! Are you all right? Did you get hurt?" What did I get? "Don't do it again." Terrific. I felt like saying, "I could use a little sympathy here!" but I didn't want to whine. A few minutes later, I fell asleep.

WEDNESDAY, DECEMBER 3

In the morning, doctors still couldn't find anything seriously amiss and they discharged me. Laura insisted on driving me to her house, where she could care for me a few days.

A hospital attendant wheeled me to the exit in a wheel-chair and Laura and the attendant helped me into her red Saturn. Satisfied that I was comfortable in the seat on the passenger side next to her, Laura revved up the Saturn and took off like a bat out of hell. She always drove like that.

She parked the Saturn in the driveway in front of her two-story woodframe house in Sylvania and I managed to get out of the car, though I was limping more than I had when I was loaded into the car. I considered suggesting that she take me back to the hospital, but I feared another ride with her at the wheel would finish me off.

The house overflowed with Christmas decorations. Laura

and her nine-year-old daughter, Kathy, were very big on celebrating the holidays, and even though Christmas was more than three weeks away, they had already decorated the house from top to bottom. An eight-foot artificial blue fir Christmas tree graced the living room, and stockings hung on the fireplace—Laura's, then Kathy's, then Country Fried's, then mine. I preferred to think this did not mean that I was lower on the pecking order than Country Fried, their terrier, but it probably did. (Like most kids, Kathy loved junk food. When it came time to name the mutt, Country Fried was the first thing that sprang to mind.)

Laura took the day off from work and allowed Kathy to stay home from school. Laura apparently thought observing someone who had sustained a high-voltage lightning surge was more educational than studying math or science. I was placed in Kathy's room—the one with teddy bear wallpaper—and Kathy was assigned to sleep on the living room sofa. I looked forward to getting a little rest, but it was not to be.

Kathy thought it would be cute to stick light bulbs into my mouth to see if they lit up. They didn't.

She asked if my hair would always have those little singed ends. I told her I didn't think so. Laura was not amused when I observed that both Laura and I had hair with split ends.

Laura made a pot of chicken noodle soup to help me "convalesce". She seemed offended when I suggested a sirloin steak might do the job better.

After lunch, Kathy asked if I had brought her any more of that "neat water" from the Miami hurricane. Her question refreshed Laura's memory about an argument Laura and I had engaged in two months earlier. When I returned from the Miami hurricane Kathy asked what I had brought her from Miami. I handed her a small plastic bottle. "Here, shrimpboat. This is genuine rain water from Hurricane Helga!"

Kathy was excited. After Kathy went to bed, Laura said it was thoughtful that in the middle of all the turmoil in Miami, I had taken the time to scoop up some water for Kathy. That's when I admitted I hadn't brought the water from Miami, I had filled the bottle with tap water out of the john at our station. "She'll never know the difference," I assured Laura. "I mean, what's the kid going to do—have it analyzed to see if it's Toledo water or Miami hurricane water?"

Well, Laura had a fit. Said it was a terrible thing to do. I responded that it was a harmless white lie, my intentions were good, and Kathy was thrilled with the water, but Laura wouldn't listen.

So, Kathy's mention of the water stirred all that up again in Laura's mind and it put a damper on things. After a few hours at Laura's house, I was going nuts. I announced my intention of returning to work immediately.

"After what you've been through—being struck by lightning!" Laura exclaimed. "The doctor said you should take two or three days off to see if there were any lingering effects."

"Aside from a craving for toasted marshmallows, I'm fine."

And so, over Laura's protests, I returned to WWTT that Wednesday afternoon. It was drizzling and cool. I tried to forget the ordeal I had been through by listening to the car radio. An AM station featured a couple of bands with a Toledo connection, We Are the Fury and Lollipop Lust Kill. That didn't do much for my fragile state of mind.

II

THE FORECAST

4

My colleagues in the WWTT newsroom couldn't resist cracking jokes about my encounter with a lightning-induced power surge.

"Look on the bright side," Brent Lassiter suggested. "You took quite a jolt and survived. If you're ever sentenced to die in the electric chair, it would take all the power in the city to kill you."

Fran mused, "it's a shame the station pays for electricity when we've got you, Jerry. You could touch a couple wires and we'd be on the air!"

Morty Greer thought her suggestion had merit.

My old buddy Dexter Bentley called from WORY. "Maybe you're in the wrong business, kid. Instead of forecasting the weather, you should be charging car batteries."

I thanked him for his concern and inquired whether he had gotten the chili stains out of his hair.

The outpouring of concern was interrupted when Pauley Sherman burst out of his office waving a memo. Pauley was easily excitable. It was probably in college that he picked up the unfortunate notion that things are supposed to run smoothly and according to some sort of plan. As a result, he was ill-prepared for the real world. Nervous by nature, Pauley tended to become rather emotional when we missed a big story, or when someone donated his favorite overcoat to the Salvation Army.

"We're in deep trouble!" he declared. "New York isn't happy!"

The corporate headquarters for Bengobar, the media conglomerate that owned WWTT, was located in New York. Every time New York sneezed, we caught colds in Toledo. Whenever the chain embarked on another belt-tightening campaign to cut expenses and increase profits, our station was in danger of being abandoned because we didn't make much money. We often received ultimatums from J.P. Bengolo, president of the corporation, but this time Pauley seemed more disturbed than usual.

"J.P. reviewed tapes of our recent newscasts and he was appalled!"

"He liked them?" asked Eric Larkin.

"No, you numbskull," Pauley growled. "He hated them! He says, and I quote, 'the rhythm, the pace, the professionalism found in the most successful broadcasts are totally lacking in yours'."

"Why doesn't he watch the other broadcasts and let us do our own thing?" Morty suggested.

"He's serious!" Pauley warned. "J.P. says if we don't turn things around, heads will roll!"

"Can't he be arrested for making threats like that?" Fran wondered.

"No. He's the boss," Morty said. "If you or I said it, we'd wind up in jail."

"So, what's the old buzzard going to do—hire more consultants to drive us nuts?" asked Brent.

J.P. periodically hired fly-by-night consultants to remedy

our ratings problems. The consultants assured us their lack of television experience was not a problem. As one of them said, "You don't need to be a chicken to know if the chicken soup is good." He did not last very long.

Another consultant recommended that the news, weather and sports anchors be stationed in front of the newsroom, thus giving viewers the impression that we have a busy, professional television news operation. Unfortunately, our reporters often left the building before the newscast hit the air, and the newsroom usually looked deserted. Instead of projecting the image of a prosperous television station, we looked as though we had just declared bankruptcy.

"He's not sending consultants," Pauley said. "I think he got tired of paying for advice like 'sell the station and buy a pizza franchise'. But he wants us to make changes. He wants improvement fast. We've got to rev up our newscasts with sensational, fast-moving reporting and great film! We're going to cover stories the whole city will be talking about! We're going to kick the other stations' butts. And one more thing . . . we're going to crank up the Happy Talk! "

The news/weather/sports team groaned.

Happy Talk is the frivolous chatter designed to make news anchors seem more human (they aren't) and push up ratings (it does). It's the glue that holds many newscasts together. Brent described it as the Slime of the News Business, noting that in films like *The Slime From Outer Space* the Slime devoured everything in its path as it grew uncontrollably, terrorizing whole populations. Our crew was having trouble with Happy Talk and the reason was obvious to me: we didn't really like each other very much.

"Don't you people realize that J.P. is doing you a favor?" Pauley pleaded. "He's trying to save your jobs! He knows the station could make more money by dropping the news operation and running 'Gilligan's Island' reruns from now till the end of time. He's trying to overhaul the news to attract more viewers, boost our ratings and give you all a more secure future!"

"What you mean," Harry Vincent grumbled, "is that the old man wants to transform the news into 'Gilligan's Island'. And we're supposed to thank the old coot for that?"

Harry, our senior reporter, had worked for television stations in Seattle, Los Angeles and Chicago until he tired of the rat race. Since he was too young to retire, he accepted a job at our little station. In his late fifties, Harry was a throwback to the old days, when men were men, news was news and entertainment was secondary.

"Cynicism is cheap," Pauley declared, "but we'll see if you're still making wisecracks when you're collecting unemployment."

"Isn't that where you get paid for not working?" Morty asked.

"That's right," Brent said. "Pauley has been collecting it for years, only he never knew it."

"You've made a mess of Happy Talk up till now," Pauley said, "but you've got no choice. You've got to make it work! I want to see you smiling, laughing and being nice to each other! . . . All right. Let's try it before you go on the air!"

Fran Rosen patted more makeup on her cheeks. Morty Greer picked his nose. I shrugged. Brent Lassiter finally said something . . .

"I gotta take a leak."

He hustled off to the men's room.

"It's really not difficult!" Pauley insisted. "Other stations take to it like a duck takes to water. How come I run the only station in the country that can't do Happy Talk?"

"How come we have the only station manager who wears his toupee backwards?" Harry Vincent mused.

"I've often wondered the same thing," I said.

"That's it!" Fran said. "That's the kind of chitchat you want, isn't it, Pauley?"

"Not exactly," Pauley grumbled.

"Sure it is," Fran continued. "We can do it. We can do Happy Talk."

Brent returned to his desk.

"All right. What shall we talk about?"

"Pauley's toupee!" Morty said enthusiastically.

"I've never understood why he wears it backwards," Brent remarked.

Pauley stomped off to his office. He was not very happy.

With trepidation, I entered my weather cubbyhole. It was the first time I had been there since the accident. I was even more leery when I realized the old Cloudchaser computer had not been replaced. I confronted Pauley in his office.

"You're so afraid to spend the station's money that you're willing to jeopardize my life!" I complained.

"You worry too much, Sheldon. The repairman said it seemed to be all right. Why spend money for a new computer when the old one still works?"

I returned to my weather cubbyhole and examined the computer closely. The sides were stained by smoke. It was singed around the edges. Yet the computer booted up all right. The first time my fingers touched the keyboard, I expected another jolt, but nothing happened. I wasn't sure why this should be so. I had been fried by a charge that flowed through the computer, but the Cloudchaser survived intact? It didn't seem fair.

In a few minutes, I was back in the swing of things, plotting high and low pressure areas, preparing a "fly-through" graphic that would show what the weather was like across our region, and trying to figure out if it had really been 114 below zero in Des Moines or if that was a typographical error.

As I worked, resentment about the ribbing I had endured smoldered in my mind. Where was the compassion, where was the concern for my health? To Brent, Fran and Morty, my Near Death Experience had been nothing but a source of amusement. And Pauley Sherman cared so little about my health and welfare he hadn't replaced the computer that fried me. Didn't they realize I had nearly been killed?

Apparently not. The sound of laughter drifted in from the newsroom. I could hear Brent talking on the telephone . . .

"But why does the *Cleveland Plain Dealer* want to do a story on Jerry Sheldon? It's not like it was the first time his brains were baked by lightning."

I suspected a few well-placed lightning jolts would knock some sense into Brent.

Pauley said, "Wait a minute! Maybe we can use this to our advantage. People will tune in to see Jerry Sheldon, the Human Lightning Rod, give the weather!"

I attempted to concentrate on my work, but I was still upset when the time came to type in the forecast for Thursday. (Since ours was a small station, I created the slides that viewers would see as I delivered the next day's forecast.) I scanned the official forecast. It warned that another storm would move into the Toledo area, dumping three or four inches of snow on Toledo. The high was expected to reach 28 degrees.

What a depressing prospect!

Annoyed by chili suppers, happy talk, the newsroom crew's lack of sympathy for my plight and the prospect of shoveling several inches of snow off my driveway, I threw caution to the wind and devised a more creative forecast . . .

> Sunny and unseasonably warm Thursday, with a high
> of 82.

I felt better already.

At 6:16 Wednesday evening, Brent Lassiter led into the weather segment:

"AND NOW, OUR OWN HIGH-VOLTAGE WEATHERMAN, JERRY SHELDON, WILL TELL US HOW IT FEELS TO BE ROASTED LIKE A CHICKEN. I'VE WONDERED ABOUT THAT FOR YEARS."

And he laughed.

"I GUESS THAT'S WHAT MAKES YOU BRENT LASSITER," I mumbled. "NORMAL PEOPLE DON'T WONDER ABOUT THINGS LIKE THAT."

I could tell Pauley Sherman wasn't listening closely because he seemed pleased we were engaging in Happy Talk. Later, he'd realize that what we said was not very friendly. For now, though, Pauley was preoccupied with other matters, such as figuring out if the station's insurance rates would skyrocket because I was fried on company time.

I launched into reporting the local stats for the day—the high was 38, the skies partly cloudy—and showed the movement of storm fronts on the weather maps. I was ready to deliver the forecast when I heard gasps from the news anchors. The forecast I had typed in anger had appeared on the Teleprompter. I decided to go with it.

"THE OFFICIAL FORECAST CALLS FOR SNOW ON THURSDAY, WITH A HIGH OF 28. WHAT A DREARY PROSPECT. SOMETIMES I WANT TO TEAR UP THE FORECAST AND SEE IF WE CAN'T COME UP WITH SOMETHING BETTER. SO WHAT DO YOU SAY? LET'S GIVE IT A TRY . . . HOW'S

THIS . . . SUNNY TOMORROW AND VERY WARM, WITH A HIGH OF 82. WHAT DO YOU THINK, BRENT?"

"THAT'S PROBABLY AS ACCURATE AS MOST OF YOUR FORECASTS," Brent responded.

I lunged at Brent just as Barb Farley cut to a commercial. I didn't intend to harm him, just perform a little brain surgery. But Eric restrained me and I cooled down.

After the commercial break, Brent happy-talked his way into Morty Greer's sports roundup.

"WHAT HAVE YOU GOT FOR US, MORTY?," Lassiter said. "HOW DID OUR BOYS DO ON THE ICE TONIGHT?"

"THE CINCINNATI CYCLONES BLEW INTO TOWN AND HANDED THE TOLEDO WALLEYE A STINGING 3-1 DEFEAT AT THE NEW DOWNTOWN ARENA," Morty grumbled. "IT WAS NOT PRETTY."

I didn't like it when sports teams had weather-related monickers, like Cyclones. Until recently, Toledo's minor league hockey franchise had been called the Toledo Storm and that really drove me nuts. When our headlines "at the top of the hour" reported "Storm Buries Roanoke" or "Storm Derailed", people never were sure if they were hearing weather bulletins or sports updates. When a real, honest-to-God, life-threatening storm bore down on Toledo, people thought we were talking about the hockey team.

Even though our hockey franchise had changed its name to the Walleye, teams like the Cincinnati Cyclones and Stockton Thunder still blew into town to play our team, and some viewers weren't sure if Morty was delivering the weather or the sports. During the baseball season, people were less likely to confuse my weather segment with Morty's sports report. Our minor league baseball team was the Toledo Mud Hens, a Detroit Tigers' farm team. When Morty reported the Mud Hens had been plucked, people didn't confuse it with the weather report. (They did confuse it with the farming report, however. And if the Mud Hens lost by a wide margin, Morty would use a stronger word that rhymed with "plucked". The Federal Communications Commission warned Morty about that. He told them to get plucked.)

On this particular evening, as Morty babbled on about the Walleye losing to the Cyclones, a wave of guilt washed over me. I shouldn't have fooled around with the weather forecast. The forecast is sacred. People depend on it. People plan their days around it. My emotions had gotten the better of me, and I had violated the sacred trust I had been charged with. I vowed to make up for it at the end of the newscast, when the news, weather and sports anchors offered a few final words before going off the air. But when it came time to close, we were running late and I didn't have time to say a word.

When our "News at 11" aired, I realized too late that the wild forecast I concocted earlier had reappeared on the monitor. I had forgotten to change it! I decided it was better to be consistent and foolish than inconsistent and foolish, so I delivered the same ridiculous forecast again.

At the end of the evening, I was not proud of myself. I vowed that if I could get through this without losing my job, I would never again screw around with the forecast.

Instead of returning to Laura's house, I headed home. I wasn't in the mood to sleep in a room decorated with teddy bear wallpaper and stuffed Ninja Turtle dolls.

It was after midnight when I parked my Buick in the drive in front of my little bungalow. I was relieved to be home. In this refuge from the cares and stresses of the world, I had created an environment uniquely suited to my needs.

Instead of filling end tables with photos of relatives, I had plastered the walls with tattered newspaper pages:

"DEAD IN A DRIFT" shouted a headline from the famous blizzard of 1888.

"INUNDATED!" declared the single-column headline in the *Kansas City Star* reporting on the Johnstown, Pennsylvania flood that killed about two thousand people in 1889.

"BABY, IT'S HOT OUTSIDE!" roared a tabloid reporting on the notorious heat wave of July, 1936.

The only memento in the living room was a piece of wood from a pier that washed away when Hurricane Andrew battered Florida.

My backyard was filled with weather instruments and a small dish which received transmissions from weather satellites. I had linked them to a Macintosh computer in my living room. I fired up the Macintosh to verify that the weather equipment was operating properly.

I was appalled to see that instrument readings indicated winds were blowing at eighty miles an hour and twenty-two inches of rain had fallen. Either we were in the midst of a helluva storm or old Hard Head McCullough, the neighbor in the shack behind me, had sabotaged my "tipping bucket" rain gauge again. He was a retired railroad worker and never seemed to do much of anything. I would get even with the old reprobate, but I'd do it some other time. It was late and I was tired.

I went to bed and within minutes, fell asleep.

III

WHO'S TURNING UP
THE HEAT?

5

That night, I dreamed Dexter Bentley had trapped me in a giant toaster and thrown the switch. I was nearly done on one side when I awoke sweating and breathing heavily.

As I climbed out of bed, I noticed the house seemed unusually warm. It should have been cool, because I always set the thermostat low at night. It could mean only one thing . . .

My house was on fire!

I dashed to the kitchen, but there was no sign of a fire anywhere. No smoke, no flames. All the appliances had been turned off.

As I headed for the bathroom, sunlight poured through a window. It was a bright, sunny day. My first reaction was that I had been screwed again. The forecast had called for low temperatures and a snowstorm. Then I remembered my flippant prediction of the evening before and laughed, because I had indeed forecast a sunny day, even though I probably had missed the high for the day by about 50 degrees.

As I was shaving, the telephone rang.

"What's happening, Jerry?"

It was Eric Larkin.

"Not much," I said. "I just got up. What's happening with you?"

"That's not what I mean. What's happening with the weather, Jerry?"

"What about the weather?"

"Have you been outside?"

"No. I figured I was doing good to make it to the bathroom."

"Go outside, then we'll talk."

I suspected Eric had been sniffing the hard stuff again, but I humored him. I donned a heavy leather jacket over my pajamas and ventured forth into the front yard.

I was stunned. It wasn't mild, it wasn't warm—it was hot! I thought it might be about 90, but I was wearing a winter coat. Something was definitely out of whack. It isn't supposed to be nice in Toledo in early December. We were supposed to suffer, like most of the country does.

Across the street, Beulah Morgan, a housewife, busily swept off her sidewalk. We had never been buddies. I don't know if it was because she was built like a fifteen-wheeler and had a personality like Tugboat Annie, or if it was because her husband had once threatened to wipe up the street with my white ass, but I didn't get along with her.

"Hey, Weatherman!" she bellowed. "It took a few years, but you finally got it right!"

She eyed me from head to toe.

"Good Lord, Weatherman. You wear pajamas with polka dots?"

A number of other people were gazing at the white pajamas with large blue polka dots. I hastily retreated to the safety of my house and picked up the phone.

"So what did you do to the weather, Jerry?" Eric asked.

"I didn't do anything! It was supposed to be cold and snowy today."

"Well, I got to thinking about it, Jerry. It's warming up fast. Probably have a high in the 80s today. That's what you predicted! I don't know how you did it, but keep up the good work! I'm going to the lakefront."

I pondered the situation and came up with only one possible explanation: I was dreaming. In a few minutes I would wake up, and poof—the nice weather would be gone and it would be 28 and snowing, just like the official forecast predicted.

I returned to bed and five minutes later got up, threw on a sweatshirt and a pair of jeans, and hustled outside. It was still hot. It was as though Toledo had been transported down to Miami Beach lock, stock and barrel, because this weather was more typical for southern Florida in early December.

"Hey, Weatherman! . . ."

Beulah Morgan's grating voice bellowed over from across the street.

". . . I like the polka dots better!"

After a quick shower, I fixed myself an egg over easy. I didn't know why the weather was screwed up, but one aspect of the situation pleased me immensely—*I* had predicted it! Not the Weather Service. Not old Dexter Bentley. Just me.

Because I handled the weather on both the 6 P.M. and 11 P.M. newscasts during the week, my workday usually began about one in the afternoon. After breakfast I drove down-town, where I intended to pick up some razor blades and explain to my bank that I hadn't really floated a bad check, I had simply erred by writing a check that had the misfor-tune to reach the bank before the funds had been processed by bank employees. Obviously, the bank had screwed up. I didn't know if the bank would buy it, but that was my story and I was sticking to it.

On the way downtown, I switched on the car radio and listened to the give-and-take between Malinda and Ralph, the most popular drive-time deejays in the city.

"Have you been outside?" a caller said. "We're havin' a heat wave! In December! What do you make of it, Malinda?"

"It's amazing. I don't think the Weather Service has any idea what's going on. The official forecast for today called for snow and a high of about 28, but I heard that Jerry Shel-don, the weatherman over at WWTT, actually predicted this hot spell last night."

"Sheldon has my vote for president," the caller said. "He knows how to get things done!"

"Well, whatever happened, let's enjoy it!" Ralph added.

After three years of handling the weather forecasts in Toledo, I was no longer surprised when people recognized me—"hey, you're that weather guy on Channel 15!"—but on this particular day, people on the streets actually seemed pleased to see me.

One middle-aged man wearing a Toledo Walleye tee shirt and shorts approached me on Cherry Street and shook my hand vigorously.

"You sure know how to call 'em!" he said. "I heard your forecast last night and I says to the wife, 'that guy is totally wacko', I mean, like, no one in his right mind says it's going to be 80 here in December, and, like everyone knew you were kinda wacko anyway for goin' down to Miami to be battered by a hurricane, but this time you did it! You finally got it together, Harry!"

"Jerry," I said. "The name is Jerry."

"What? Oh, yeah. Jerry. Well, keep up the good work, Jer. Is it going to be warm like this tomorrow?"

"I have no idea. I haven't looked at the weather charts yet."

"See what you can do, Jer. I'd like to squeeze in a round of golf before the next snowstorm hits. Did you ever try banging in a twenty-foot putt when a foot of snow blankets the green? It's not easy."

I headed off to the bank, where I explained to a bank official named Mrs. Kellstadt that I had not really written a bad check, and so forth. She said she understood the situation perfectly. Then she slapped a twenty-dollar charge on me for passing a bad check and added a note to my account reporting my delinquency. I had the feeling that if I ever wrote a bad check again, I would be making license plates in a state prison for five or ten years.

What was this strange effect I had on women like Mrs. Kellstadt, Beulah Morgan and my fianceé? It was as though I wore skunk oil aftershave.

After lunch at the Aztec Grille on SeaGate, I headed for the television station. Perhaps the weather data would help me determine what had happened.

Dozens of people were strolling, jogging and playing softball along the lakefront and in nearby parks. They wore summer clothes—shorts and short-sleeve shirts and blouses—and there was an electricity in the air that usually was lacking in December.

In the WWTT newsroom, my colleagues eyed me with strange expressions, half "wow, how'd you do that?" and half "what kind of weirdo are you, anyway?"

Brent Lassiter, never one to beat around the bush, demanded, "What the hell did you do to the weather, Sheldon?"

"I haven't the faintest idea," I said.

"Maybe we should all get struck by lightning," Morty Greer suggested.

"In your case, it couldn't hurt," I pointed out.

Fran Rosen tagged along as I headed for my weather cubbyhole. "The really strange thing about this," she noted, "is that a few miles outside of town, a blizzard is raging and the temperature is about 25 degrees. How is that possible, Jerry?"

"Let me check the weather data and I'll get back to you on that," I said. Translation: I hadn't the faintest idea.

One thing was obvious: people would watch our broadcast that evening to hear me explain what had happened. I needed to put together some sort of explanation that sounded plausible, even if it was totally off the wall.

Weather maps, temperature reports and barometric pressure readings led me to one conclusion: there was no logical reason for our abnormally blissful weather. Fran was right: fifteen miles in any direction, a snowstorm raged and people were freezing their buns off. How could Toledo be enjoying temperatures in the 80s and clear skies?

It's true that areas very close together can have radically different weather. Let's say a giant snowstorm is moving east and it's dumping a load on Bismarck, North Dakota. But the storm hasn't reached Jamestown, North Dakota, and

Jamestown is still under the effects of a warm front, so it's sunny and 40 degrees warmer.

As I studied weather maps on the Cloudchaser computer, however, I noticed there was no such movement of fronts, although a warm front had inexplicably settled over Toledo.

I recalled that once when I visited Albuquerque, New Mexico, an overnight snowstorm dumped nineteen inches of snow in the foothills of the Sandia Mountains, on the outskirts of the city, while other parts of the city received only two or three inches of snow. That vast differential could be explained primarily by the difference in altitude. I could find no geographical rationale for our strange weather.

I wondered if human weather-makers had screwed up the weather through cloud seeding or some other device, inadvertently creating a warm front over Toledo. There was ample evidence weather-makers had screwed up the weather over the years, but there was no evidence this had happened over Toledo in the last twenty-four hours.

"Heat bursts" can raise temperatures 25 or 30 degrees in just a few minutes, but these occur only under rare conditions after thunderstorms and last a short time—perhaps a half hour or so.

Lake Effect Snow often dropped snowfall on cities along the Great Lakes when other areas didn't have any snow. Perhaps the reverse was happening—the lake was bringing us hot weather while the rest of the region shivered. But that didn't make any sense.

I was running out of explanations. Perhaps I should admit it was a fluke, some sort of weird, one-in-a-billion weather phenomenon. I could tell viewers I knew of no plausible explanation why Toledo should be enjoying good weather when our neighbors were being pummeled by a snowstorm. That was not really a viable alternative, however. For a weatherman to admit he had no idea what was happening to the weather was like a congressman conceding he had no idea what was going on in Washington. True, but very unprofessional.

The whole thing was very disconcerting. One of the comforting things about weather forecasting is that there is order in the weatherman's universe. The meterologist might miss something and screw up an occasional forecast, but forecasting is based on atmospheric conditions that are familiar and predictable. If things do not act in an orderly fashion—if they are chaotic or random—the weather forecaster's job would be impossible. On this day, in Toledo, the weather had been chaotic and unpredictable, and weather forecasters were bewildered. We had lost our security blanket, the orderliness that made us feel warm and secure and comfortable.

I checked my "voice mail"—the euphemism used to describe messages left on our telephone answering machine system—and discovered W.C. Muldoon had phoned and asked that I return his call.

W.C. Muldoon—the W.C. stood for Wind Chill—was a cantankerous old buzzard who happened to be a bigshot at the local Weather Service facility. He was the Godfather of Toledo weather. He didn't have Mafia connections, but he had his fingers in all the pots; he kept close tabs on the close-knit fraternity of Toledo weathermen. I hadn't had occasion to talk to W.C. since he informed me that he had monitored my telecasts for the National Meteorological Society and because I had done stupid things like weather remotes from chili suppers, I had been barred from membership in the Meteorological Society. For life. I asked why Dexter Bentley had been allowed into the N.M.S. He did remotes from chili suppers all the time. "Dexter's like family," W.C. told me. "You're like the family dog."

I called the Weather Service and waited for W.C. to get to the phone. I could hear him talking on another line . . . "Look, I don't know what's happening to the weather here. . . . Yes, I know how stupid the weather maps look when there's a small warm front sitting smack in the middle of a blizzard, but I don't make the weather, I just report it! . . . I'm trying to get a handle on this. I've got a joker on the other line who might know something about it. I'll get back to you."

A few moments later, W.C. clicked in on my line. "Sheldon, what's going on? How do you explain our weather today?"

"I can't," I said. "I have no idea what happened. I forecast it as a joke last night and today, voilá . . . our weather is like Florida's. That's all I know, W.C."

"Listen, you arrogant little punk—"

Good grief, I thought. Was that any way for a professional weatherman to talk to a colleague?

"—we've had our eyes on you for some time—"

Maybe they were going to let me into the Meteorological Society.

"—and you've been doing some pretty weird stuff—"

Apparently not.

"—like that incident last summer when you did a remote from a swimming pool on the hottest day of the year—"

That had been Brent Lassiter's idea.

"—and WWTT's remote truck backed into the pool, nearly killing a half dozen kids—"

Eric Larkin had forgotten to apply the parking brake

when he parked the truck at the edge of the pool. It wasn't my fault!

"—and of course there was your showboating during the devastating Miami hurricane—"

I wasn't showboating! I risked my life to report what was happening!

"—and now this, where you predict that it's going to be 82 degrees here, even though a major snowstorm is headed this way, and you turn out to be right. I've got quite a file on you, Sheldon, and I'm considering taking legal action against you."

"For what?" I demanded. "For accurately predicting a warm spell, you arrogant fool! How would it look if you sue me for issuing an accurate forecast? You'd be laughed out of the business!"

"You're dangerous, Sheldon, and I'm going to keep a close eye on you."

He paused. When he resumed talking, his tone had softened noticeably. "Could you tell me how this happened? How did you do it?"

"Witchcraft," I said.

"I knew it! I knew it had to be something like that!"

And he hung up.

I was in the midst of preparing a slide listing the high temperatures in major cities when the phone rang again.

"What did you do to screw up the weather, kid?"

It was Dexter Bentley.

"You think I created this weather? Do you realize how crazy that sounds, Dexter?"

"You forecast it. You must have had something to do with it. How did you know it was going to be hot? And why is a snowstorm dropping a load on towns just outside the city while we roast in this heat?"

"Dexter, you're losing it. You sound like a mental hospital dropout. I had nothing to do with it. I'm just a weatherman, like you. Don't you know anything about isobars, barometric pressure and squaw lines?"

"Why, you little runt. I've forgotten more about them than you'll ever know!"

Was that supposed to be a point in his favor?

"I don't know what you're up to, kid, but when I find out, you'll be in a lot of trouble."

Pauley Sherman barged into my weather cubicle carrying a package.

"Our forecast beat the other stations and the Weather Service by a mile! How did you do it, Sheldon?"

"I don't know. It was a lucky guess."

"The hell it was. Do you realize the ramifications of this? This weather thing could be dynamite! We can exploit it for all it's worth, and then some. Let's put our heads together and brainstorm on this . . . hmm . . . how about 'WWTT—Your Fair Weather Station'. What do you think?"

"I don't know, Pauley . . ."

"You're right. It sounds like they can't count on us when the weather turns bad. We need to blow our own horns a little. . . . I don't hear you coming up with any suggestions, Sheldon. Put your brain in high gear!"

"How about 'WWTT—First in Weather'," I suggested.

"Dullsville, Sheldon. Besides, it reminds people by implication that we're last in news. . . . How about 'WWTT—the Miracle Weather Station!' I love it! We'll use it during all our station breaks. How do I come up with these things?"

"Pauley, it doesn't seem right to exploit something like this. I told you—it was just a lucky guess."

"You've got a lot to learn about the cutthroat world of business. My mother put me through college running a flower shop. When I was able to start my own string of flower shops, I drove her grubby little shop into the ground. There's no room for sentimentality in business, Sheldon. We're under a lot of pressure to boost our ratings. We can't let this opportunity slip through our fingers. We'll milk it for all it's worth. Your forecast wasn't a lucky guess—it was a miracle!"

I groaned.

I reached into my desk and handed Pauley a form I had filled out.

"What's this?" he mumbled, glancing at it.

"A request for reimbursement of travel expenses."

"In the first place, Sheldon, you must itemize expenses and turn in mileage and receipts. You can't just write 'One hurricane. One thousand three hundred dollars and twenty-six cents'. The Business Department and the I.R.S. are sticklers about little things like that. In the second place, I told you before you left for Florida that the station wouldn't pay your expenses. You ran off to Miami on your own."

"It was worth a try," I mumbled.

Pauley dropped the package he was holding on my desk.

"By the way, this quilt came in the mail. A ninety-three-year-old woman in Perrysburg knitted it. Show it on the air tonight and thank the old gal for sending it to us."

I leaned back in my chair and glared. "Pauley, weathermen don't plug quilts. They did that kind of thing on television years ago, but not anymore. It's like chili suppers and picking your nose. It's a no-no."

"Do you like working here, Sheldon?"

Pauley was trying to exercise raw power. I could play hardball, too.

"No."

"Well, you've got a choice. You can be unhappy and employed, or unhappy and unemployed. … Take care of the quilt for me, Jer."

As Pauley left, I wondered if he had given me all the choices. Why couldn't I be happy and unemployed? I could be if I had a lot of money in the bank, but I didn't. It appeared I had no choice but to be unhappy and employed.

Thanks to W.C. Muldoon, Dexter Bentley, Pauley Sherman and a little old lady in Perrysburg, I was again feeling moody and irritable when it came time to type in the forecast on my Cloudchaser computer. Once more, I threw caution to the wind and forecast another day of sunny skies and unusually high temperatures, with a high of 84. And I even added a little footnote to the forecast for the little old lady in Perrysburg.

6

When the "WWTT News at 6" aired that Thursday evening, Brent Lassiter immediately tackled the topic everyone was talking about . . . the summer-like temperatures which took Toledo by surprise. The weather was the lead story, something that usually happened only after a tornado or devastating storm ripped through the city.

"THE BIG QUESTION EVERYONE IS ASKING IS: HOW DID THIS HAPPEN?" Brent asserted in his authoritative broadcasting voice that made him sound like a cross between Walter Cronkite and Mickey Mouse. Film of Toledoans enjoying the unseasonably warm weather appeared on the monitor. "WHY DID TOLEDO HAVE CLEAR SKIES TODAY WITH A HIGH OF 82 DEGREES WHEN FIFTEEN MILES IN ANY DIRECTION IT WAS 60 DEGREES COOLER AND SNOWING? LET'S ASK JERRY SHELDON, WHO WAS THE ONLY WEATHERMAN TO FORECAST THIS AMAZING CHANGE IN TOLEDO'S WEATHER. WHAT ABOUT IT, JERRY? HOW DID IT HAPPEN?"

Brent was showing no mercy. I was on the spot. I decided to take a page out of the politicians' book: seduce people with dazzling images and meaningless rhetoric and maybe they won't notice you don't know what you're talking about. I would emphasize what was happening and downplay the fact I didn't know *why* it was happening.

"WHAT IT ALL BOILS DOWN TO IS THAT I DETECTED A BREAK IN THE STORM PATTERN THAT NO ONE ELSE FORESAW. . . ."

If you believe that, I've got a '77 Ford I'll sell you for twenty grand.

". . . THE CONDITIONS THAT BROUGHT ABOUT THE HIGH TEMPERATURES TODAY WERE A FLUKE, AN EXTRAORDINARY, ONE-IN-A-MILLION SITUATION. AS YOU'LL SEE BY THE WEATHER MAP, THE LOW PRESSURE THAT'S FEEDING THE SNOWSTORM IS ENTRENCHED ALL AROUND US, BUT IT'S BYPASSING TOLEDO JUST AS IT WOULD IF TOLEDO WERE ENCLOSED IN A HUGE DOME. IT'S NOT UNUSUAL FOR TWO PLACES THAT ARE RELATIVELY CLOSE TO HAVE COMPLETELY DIFFERENT WEATHER, BUT THE TYPE OF EXTREME, LOCALIZED VARIATION IN THE WEATHER WE EXPERIENCED TODAY IS VERY RARE.

"THE WEATHER SERVICE SAYS THE HIGH PRESSURE CELL THAT FORMED HERE AND RESULTED IN THIS TERRIFIC, SUMMER-LIKE WEATHER WILL BE LONG GONE BY TOMORROW. I'LL GIVE YOU *MY* FORECAST IN A FEW MINUTES."

That was followed by other news reports.

It would be several minutes before viewers realized I hadn't answered Brent's question about *why* our weather had gone bonkers. And I figured Brent never would.

At 6:16, Fran led into my weather segment.

"WHERE DID YOU FIND THAT BEAUTIFUL QUILT?" she asked. I took the cue.

"NINETY-THREE-YEAR-OLD FLORENCE BODECKER OF PERRYSBURG SENT US THIS QUILT. IT TOOK HER EIGHT MONTHS TO PATCH IT TOGETHER. STATION MANAGER PAULEY SHERMAN WAS OVERWHELMED, FLO. HE THINKS IT'S A GOSH-DARN WONDERFUL QUILT."

I could hear Pauley gasping for air in the Control Booth. He was not amused. I ran down the weather statistics—it was the first time I had given a "heat index" in December— and showed more weather graphics. Soon, it was time for

Friday's forecast. The Weather Service was predicting snow and low temperatures again, but the forecast I had typed on the computer earlier came up on the monitor, and I decided to go with it.

"The official forecast isn't very exciting—snow and cold, and all that dreary stuff. What do you say, gang? Should we go for it again? All right! Friday, look for mostly sunny skies with light breezes and a high of 84. But in Perrysburg, it's going to be a different story. I tell you what, Flo. I'm going to send the quilt back to you because you're going to need it. A ferocious winter blizzard is going to sweep down on you tomorrow."

Fran shook her head. "The official forecast calls for a high of 27 in Toledo. Do you really think it will be 84?"

"Let's hope for the best," I said.

As we cut to a commercial, reality began to sink in. I had done it again. I could easily have delivered the official forecast, but no, not me. I manufactured a completely ridiculous prognostication. Coincidence had made a hero out of me the first time—I had predicted it would be in the 80s, and because of some unexplainable phenomenon, it had been—but there was no way it would happen again. I felt like a compulsive gambler who wins a big pot playing roulette and then, instead of cashing in his chips, places another bet—and lets it all ride on Number 84.

WWTT tapes the newscasts of the other Toledo stations. After our news went off the air that evening, I viewed the tape of Dexter Bentley's weathercast over at Channel 28. I was anxious to see how the self-proclaimed "Dean of Toledo Weathermen" would explain what was going on.

"What about the extraordinarily warm day we had today?"

Channel 28 co-anchor Bessie Thornball asked Dexter. "WHAT IN THE WORLD CAUSED IT?"

Dexter smiled confidently. "THE HOLE IN THE OZONE LAYER," he declared.

"THE OZONE LAYER?" Bessie repeated, in bewilderment.

I was stunned.

"THAT'S RIGHT," Dexter continued. "AS YOU MAY KNOW, FLUO-ROCARBONS AND OTHER JUNK HAVE CREATED A HOLE IN THE ATMO-SPHERE THAT IS ALLOWING MORE OF THE SUN'S ULTRAVIOLET RAYS TO PENETRATE OUR ATMOSPHERE, RESULTING IN A WARMING UP OF OUR CLIMATE—THE 'GLOBAL WARMING' YOU HEAR ABOUT ON TALK SHOWS. TODAY, THE HOLE WAS DIRECTLY OVER TOLEDO. SUNLIGHT BURNED THROUGH THE CLOUDS OVER TOLEDO—AND ONLY OVER TOLEDO—ALLOWING US TO HAVE SUNNY SKIES AND A HOT DAY WHEN ALL AROUND US, PEOPLE WERE BATTLING A BLIZZARD."

Dexter's explanation was completely off-the-wall, of course, but I had to hand it to him. I thought he had never heard of the ozone layer, and here he was pontificating about it on television. Later, a reporter at WORY told me what had happened. Dexter, completely baffled by the sudden change in the weather, desperately searched for a plausible expla-nation, and when the old con artist washed up before the broadcast, he picked up a can of aerosol hairspray and was about to spray it on his disgusting head of graying hair when the notation on the label caught his eye. It stated that the can contained no harmful fluorocarbons that would contribute to the deterioration of the ozone layer. Dexter's inventive little mind said, "That's it!"

Not only was Dexter's explanation totally absurd, he apparently forgot to use the spray, because he was having a Bad Hair Day.

That evening, I drove over to Laura's house and was disappointed to realize she wanted to talk about the weather, too.

"It's not normal to have 80-degree temperatures in Toledo in early December, Jerry, and I don't mind telling you that I don't like you going around predicting it. It's like you actually created the weather. You're trampling on God's turf. I just want you to know: if you're fooling around with the occult, I won't have anything to do with you, and neither will Kathy. I'll call off the wedding."

I reached inside the refrigerator for a beer, but came out with a bottle of mineral water.

"What happened to the six-pack I brought over the other day?"

Laura shrugged. "I decided it wasn't a good idea to have beer in the refrigerator when there's a nine-year-old child in the house. Besides, I finished it off this afternoon when I discovered it was 82 outside, just like you predicted."

"There's nothing to get upset about," I assured Laura, as we snuggled up together on the sofa. "I delivered a ridiculous weather forecast and it happened to come true. That's all that happened. Nothing occult about it, nothing smacking of the Devil, no Ouija board. Just dumb luck."

Laura smiled. "I'm glad to hear it." She ran her hands through my hair. "Do you think it had something to do with lightning striking you? Maybe the voltage put you in touch with weird cosmic forces."

"The only weird cosmic forces I've been in touch with come from the Internal Revenue Service. Incidentally, they said they were much amused by my new system of 'creative accounting' and they'd like to talk with me about it in the very near future. Since you filled out my returns, I think you should be there. Pack a bag. You might be going away for three-to-five years. Don't worry about the kid. I'll give her all the mineral water she can drink."

"Jerry ... I did your taxes as a favor to you!"

"I know, and I appreciate it." I kissed her. "Next year, if you're sitting in the klink somewhere, I'm going to have Dexter Bentley do my taxes."

She chuckled. "Isn't he weird. 'The ozone layer'. What an imagination!"

I looked at her in astonishment. "You watched Dexter's weather instead of mine? Why?"

"He's the Dean of Toledo Weathercasters."

"I'm getting out of here. You aren't Laura. What did you do with Laura?"

"Relax. I was kidding. I taped Dexter on my VCR and watched it after you were finished. Jerry, I can understand why you made up a forecast yesterday. You were irritated with the nitwits at the station and people who blamed you for the weather. But I don't understand why you forecast temperatures in the 80s for tomorrow, too."

"I just had the feeling I should."

"What if being struck by lightning gave you some sort of power to actually create weather. Whatever you predict comes true . . ."

"That's ridiculous. It was just coincidence."

"But what if I'm right?"

I thought a moment."Well, if you're right, I wouldn't want to be old Florence Bodecker. I predicted great weather for us, but I sent a blizzard her way."

"I forgot about that!"

"I shouldn't have done it, but it doesn't matter, because I don't have any control over the weather."

"All I know, Jerry, is that you had better stop messing around with things like the weather! It's not right!"

"I agree entirely. Now, why don't you and I go in the bedroom and mess around."

I heard a little voice from the hallway.

"Hi, Jerry!" Kathy was wearing a nightie and had that sleepy look a person has when they've just woken up. She headed toward the kitchen and poured herself a glass of milk. "What are you doing here?"

"Just messing around," I said.

She jumped up on the couch, squeezing between Laura and me. "I'm glad you're here. We were talking about the weather in school, and I told the other kids you were going to be my father and that you knew everything about the weather. So why was it so hot today?"

It looked like Laura and I wouldn't be able to do any messing around, so I proceeded to lecture Kathy on the facts of life about high pressure cells and tropical heat waves. Later, I drove to my house.

7

I awoke the next morning with ambivalent feelings. On the one hand, I hoped my forecast of a continuing heat wave for Toledo would come true. On the other, if I had some mysterious power to create weather and a blizzard swept down on Florence Bodecker's house, the old broad might come looking for me—and I never trust ninety-three-year-old women who play with needles.

Little beads of sweat on my forehead suggested it was warm in the house. I slipped on a wrinkled blue bathrobe and shabby slippers and ventured outside. Sure enough, it was another hot day, the kind that made you want to call your boss and tell him you were sick—and then head for the beach. Other weather forecasters had missed the mark by about 50 degrees. I had nailed it again. I felt like the Michael Jordan of weather forecasting. I had slam-dunked the weather down old Dexter Bentley's throat!

I turned on my heels and was returning to the house when Beulah Morgan bellowed from across the street . . .

"Hey, Weatherman! What's the matter—don't you own any street clothes?"

Apparently she didn't like my bathrobe any better than she did my pajamas.

Safely back in the house, I flipped on my television and listened to "American Horizons", one of the network morning shows, as I fixed myself a couple frozen waffles and orange juice. Ollie Jenkins, the weatherman on "American Horizons", offered congratulations to old-timers who had just turned a hundred, then launched into the weather.

"HOLY TOLEDO! WHAT'S HAPPENING IN TOLEDO, OHIO? IT REACHED 82 DEGREES THERE YESTERDAY, AND THEY SEEM TO BE HEADED FOR ANOTHER HOT DAY—BUT EVERYWHERE NEAR TOLEDO, FIERCE WINTER STORMS ARE RAGING. I DON'T MIND TELLING YOU THAT METEOROLOGISTS ARE PERPLEXED. THERE'S NO LOGICAL EXPLANATION. DID A WEATHER MANIPULATION EXPERIMENT GO AWRY? DID SOME NATURAL PHENOMENON SPAWN A HIGH PRESSURE CELL OVER TOLEDO? WE JUST DON'T KNOW. ALL WE KNOW FOR SURE IS THAT THE FINE FOLKS IN CLEVELAND AND AKRON ARE WEARING HEAVY COATS AND SNOW BOOTS TODAY, WHILE TOLEDOANS ARE STROLLING AROUND IN SHORTS AND RUNNING THEIR AIR CONDITIONERS."

I checked the readings from the weather instruments in my backyard and was shocked to learn that the thermometer which measured the maximum temperature had recorded a high of 138 degrees. It was hot, but I knew it wasn't that hot. Old Hard Head McCullough had struck again.

I stomped out to my back porch and hollered. *"McCullough! Hey, you old fossil!"*

The grizzly old hulk opened a window at the rear of his house. "Whatdyawant, Weatherman?"

"I told you to stop messing with my weather instruments! What did you do to my thermometer?"

He chuckled. "How do I know what happened? I just mind my own business."

It was then I noticed old Hard Head had repositioned his clothes dryer vent. Escaping heat blew directly on my thermometer.

"Move that damn thing, you crazy old buzzard!" I hollered. *"If you do that again, I'm going to get a hose and funnel the hot air back into your house. It'll be 138 inside your house!"*

The ringing of the phone interrupted our neighborly conversation. Eric Larkin called to say he had been assigned to shoot video around Toledo and the suburbs portraying the startling contrast in weather conditions. He invited me to go along. I hesitated because Eric had a reputation as being a little off-the-wall. Office scuttlebutt had it that his favorite movie was *Psycho* and his favorite color was "blood red". I don't know why our Personnel Department didn't pick up on little things like that before people were hired. Nevertheless, I agreed to go along.

At 9:30, Eric showed up in his Red Mustang. He was dressed for summer—a white "Beach Bum" tee shirt and blue shorts.

"Ready to boogie, Jerry?"

"I never boogie before noon," I grumbled.

"This weather is great, but it's weird. We're getting reports that hotels all over the city are booked up because people are flocking here from areas in the path of snowstorms."

When we arrived at Olander Park in suburban Sylvania, Eric leaped out of the car and started shooting video of shapely young women in bikinis that left very little to the imagination. The water hadn't warmed up much, but I had the feeling the young beauties had come to the park more for fun than swimming.

"How did you do it, Jerry?" Eric asked, as he focused on a buxom nineteen-year-old co-ed. "You can tell me."

"I don't know how I did it. And that's the truth. I don't even know *if* I did it."

"Was it the lightning? If it was, I might sit under a tree the next time there's a thunderstorm."

"I wouldn't recommend it. Lightning is supposed to be seven times hotter than the surface of the sun."

Eric had the shots he wanted, but he pretended he was still shooting because he wanted to ogle the voluptuous young women a little longer. "That's right, honey. Let it all hang out. That's great . . . Maybe you'd better give me your phone number in case this doesn't turn out and I need to re-shoot it." He directed his conversation at me again: "Perhaps it has something to do with the lightning being filtered through a computer before it fried you."

"Perhaps. But I wouldn't sit in front of a live computer waiting for lightning to strike, either. Lightning can blow the brains out of a computer."

Our next stop was suburban Perrysburg. Eric put more film in his camera and insisted on shooting video of Florence Bodecker's house, since I had singled out Mrs. Bodecker for attention. As we entered Perrysburg off Interstate 475, we noticed mounds of snow that snow removal trucks had piled up along the roads. A half dozen cars had been abandoned. Heavy snow was still falling. And five minutes away it was 80 degrees!

Eric's Mustang slid over the slickened streets.

"Here it is," he said. "Sommerwalk Street. And that house over there must be where Mrs. Bodecker lives."

We stared in amazement. Two-foot drifts of snow surrounded the house. Eight inches of the white stuff had accumulated on the sidewalks and lawn. Icicles hung from the windows.

"You ought to be ashamed of yourself, Jerry," Eric said. "She's ninety-three years old, and there's a blizzard raging. She's stranded in her house!"

"Well, she's got plenty of time to work on her quilts," I pointed out.

Eric grimaced. "You ought to be more sympathetic."

He jumped out of the car to shoot video of Mrs. Bodecker's house, but he didn't stay out of the car long because he was still wearing a tee shirt and shorts.

"I think I saw her peeking out of a window on the first floor," Eric said, as he scrambled back into the car. "She was holding something . . . quilting needles or a gun. I'm not sure which."

"Let's get out of here!" I declared.

"Maybe we ought to shovel off her sidewalk."

"No! If we do it once, she'll expect us to do it every time there's a little snow. The exercise will do her good."

I don't know why I said that. I usually treat senior citizens with respect and try to be helpful. It was nothing personal, because I had never met Florence Bodecker. It had to be that confounded quilt, and Pauley Sherman's insistence I plug it on my weather segment.

Within minutes, we fled the horrors of winter and hightailed it back to tropical Toledo.

"If we figure out how you did this," Eric mused, "we could patent it, bottle it and become billionaires!"

"You don't patent the weather," I insisted. "God wouldn't be too happy about that. Besides, if it were possible, AT&T would have done it already. There would be an extra charge on our bills every month. 'Weather from November 21 to December 21—thirty dollars and twenty-eight cents.' And a twenty per cent surcharge for sunny days."

By the time we arrived at the WWTT parking lot, the snow from Perrysburg had melted off Eric's car.

As Eric and Barb Farley edited the videotape, I poured over weather data on my Cloudchaser computer. How could I explain such abnormally high temperatures for a second day? I couldn't claim it was a freak of nature—a million-to-one shot—two days in a row. People expected more of their television weatherman.

I was scrutinizing barometer readings from the northwest suburbs when Pauley Sherman wandered into my weather cubbyhole. "It's just amazing," he mumbled. "Look at this!"

In his hands was a copy of that morning's *Toledo Blade*. The *Blade*, which had been founded in 1835, was a full-size paper, not a tabloid, though it was not as large and unwieldy in format as it had been in 1875 when the *American Journalist* commented, "The weather is too cold to read it in the apple orchard, and the paper is too large to unfold in any ordinary house in Ohio." At one time it had been known as the home paper of David Ross Locke, the humorist who created "Petroleum V. Nasby".

My eyes were drawn to the banner headline:

TOLEDO SWEATS AS OHIO SHIVERS
Summer-Like Weather
Stuns Meteorologists

The story described the incredible weather and quoted the mayor, who appeared to be claiming it as one of the achievements of his administration: "I hope people remember who was mayor when this wonderful weather came to Toledo," he declared. A color photo showed the activity at the riverfront, while a page one sidebar noted that I was the only weatherman to predict the stunning change in temperatures. The reporter compared my achievement to Babe Ruth's "calling his shot", when the King of Swat pointed to the stands and then belted a home run there.

The reporter also had interviewed W.C. Muldoon at the Weather Service about my achievement—"It's not possible for anyone to predict such a fluke in the weather; I don't care if you do have it on videotape!"—and three television weathermen, including Dexter Bentley, who suggested "the kid over at WWTT is always screwing up the forecast. The high was supposed to be 28 degrees. The kid probably misread it and said the high would be 82, and when it happened to get up into the 80s the next day, everyone thought he predicted it. The kid's a menace." Apparently the reporter called WWTT to talk to me, but someone told him I had left for Pakistan to cover the monsoons. My guess would be that the *Blade* reporter had talked to Brent.

"This is great publicity!" Pauley said. "Everyone will watch our newscast tonight. We'll have our highest ratings in history! Keep up the good work, Jer. . . . Oh, by the way, Monday you'll be doing a remote from a benefit car wash in Maumee."

"Wrong!" I said.

Pauley plopped his rump on my desk, knocking half the papers to the floor. "Don't play games with me, Sheldon. You've got to do it. It's part of your job!"

I decided to use my new-found leverage.

"No problem. I'll quit. There are a hundred stations who would pay me a lot more money than you are."

Pauley turned pale. "You can't quit! You've got a contract."

"Which is up in two weeks," I reminded him.

Pauley sighed deeply. "All right, Sheldon. What do you want?"

"No more chili suppers, no more fish frys, no more car washes. If I do any remotes it will be because the weather warrants it, not because you want me to be a clown. I won't do anything that humiliates me or diminishes my dignity and integrity as a meteorologist!"

"What dignity and integrity? Last summer I caught you dropping water bombs on Brent and Morty. Your job is to read the forecast. You're not Edward R. Murrow!"

"Maybe I'll take a job at one of the other stations in town. That way, I'd be competing against you, and I could run you into the ground every chance I get."

Pauley gritted his teeth. "All right." He turned to leave. "No more chili suppers or car wash remotes."

"I'm not done with you!" I barked.

Pauley halted abruptly. When he faced me, he was glaring. "Don't push your luck, Sheldon. I knew you when you were just a punk weatherman without any clout. That was two days ago. This heat wave won't last forever, and when it ends, you'll be just a punk again."

"That's why I want it in writing now. I also want another minute of airtime every night and a bigger weather budget!"

"We can't do that," Pauley grumbled.

"If you don't meet my requests, I'm going to come down with the flu tonight. It would be a shame to disappoint all these people who tune in to watch the weather."

Pauley sighed heavily. "I liked you better when you feared me because I'm the boss."

"I never feared you because you're the boss," I pointed out. "I feared you because you're a scheming, paranoid little ass-kisser. You're dangerous!"

"There! That's what I'm talking about! What happened to that wonderful working relationship we had?"

"It's over, Pauley. From now on, things are going to be different."

Pauley was in a much more somber mood when he left my weather cubicle.

8

Toledo's mysterious weather bugged me as much as it did Dexter, W.C. and most Toledoans. I was at the heart of whatever was happening, but I had no clue about what was really going on. The mystery finally began to unravel later that afternoon. When I fired up the Cloudchaser computer to prepare graphics for the 6 P.M. newscast, a message filled the screen:

```
ARE YOU HAVING FUN PLAYING WITH THE WEATHER,
HOT SHOT?
```

Since the message seemed to be meant for me, I punched out an answer on my computer keyboard. As I typed, the words appeared on the monitor.

```
Who is this?
NONE OF YOUR BUSINESS. LET'S JUST SAY I CON-
TROLLED TOLEDO'S WEATHER UNTIL WE DECIDED TO
LET YOU HAVE A WHIRL AT IT.
```

I figured someone at the Weather Service was playing a joke on me.

> Is that you, W.C.? Are you trying to mess with my mind, you old goat?
> WHO IS W.C.? THERE'S NO ONE UP HERE NAMED W.C.
> What do you mean 'up here'?
> YOU CALL IT HEAVEN. FOR ME, IT'S THE OLD HOME-STEAD.
> What are you telling me? Are you God?
> NO. WHAT DO YOU THINK--GOD HAS NOTHING TO DO BUT SIT AROUND SENDING YOU MESSAGES ON A COMPUTER? IN THE OLD DAYS HE HANDLED THE WEATHER HIMSELF--THE 40 DAYS OF RAIN, THE FEROCIOUS HAIL THAT POUNDED EGYPT, MAJOR PROJECTS LIKE THAT. NOW HE LETS ME TAKE CARE OF THE WEATHER, MORE OR LESS. YOU CAN CALL ME EDWARD.

I was still sure it was some joker at the Weather Service. If someone in Heaven wanted to communicate with me, I figured they'd use a burning bush or a plague of locusts to get my attention, not a weather computer.

> So your name is Edward and you are in Heaven . . .
> How do I know you're telling the truth?
> DID YOU FORECAST THAT IT WOULD BE 82 DEGREES IN TOLEDO YESTERDAY? AND WAS IT?
> That could be coincidence.
> AND YOU SAID IT WOULD BE 84 TODAY. IS IT?
> Another coincidence.
> IF I SAY I'M GOING TO FRY YOUR BRAIN AGAIN WITH ANOTHER LIGHTNING STRIKE, AND I DO IT RIGHT NOW, WOULD THAT BE A COINCIDENCE?
> Let's not find out.

For someone in Heaven, Edward had a nasty streak. If Edward was truly Up There, the lightning strike had somehow linked my computer to the Hereafter. I could only hope any connection charges were going on Edward's bill, not mine.

> Are you really putting me in charge of the weather?

> I GET TIRED OF HEARING HOT SHOTS LIKE YOU COM-PLAIN ABOUT HOW ANYONE COULD DO A BETTER JOB WITH IT THAN ME. SO THIS IS YOUR CHANCE TO CONTROL TOLEDO'S WEATHER, SPORT. PUT UP OR SHUT UP.

I didn't want to appear arrogant or egotistical, but this was a cinch. A win-win situation. If I had the power to schedule weather, what could possibly go wrong? This was my ticket to a better job, fame, fortune—and socks without holes in them!

> How does this work? Will any weather forecast I type on this machine come to pass?

> I LIKE THAT PHRASE 'COME TO PASS'. WE USED IT A LOT IN THE BIBLE.

> You didn't give me an answer.

> MAYBE IT WILL COME TO PASS. WE'RE NOT SURE IF YOU CAN HANDLE THE WEATHER. THIS IS LIKE A JOB TRYOUT. IN THE MAJOR LEAGUES, THEY CALL IT SPRING TRAINING. WE'LL SEE WHAT HAPPENS FOR A MONTH AND GO FROM THERE. WE'LL SEE IF YOU HAVE WHAT IT TAKES TO MAKE THE TEAM, OR IF YOU'LL BE A MINOR LEAGUER ALL YOUR LIFE. RIGHT NOW YOU CONSIDER YOURSELF HOT STUFF. THE NEXT BABE RUTH OF WEATHER FORECASTING. YOU GIVE PEOPLE HOT WEATHER IN DECEMBER AND THEY THINK YOU'RE TER-RIFIC. WELL, IT'S NOT THAT EASY, KID. THE WEATHER IS A LOT MORE COMPLICATED THAN THAT.

> I get the feeling you're not happy with this arrangement.

ALL RIGHT, I ADMIT IT. IT WASN'T MY IDEA. MY SUPERIORS HEARD YOU COMPLAINING ABOUT THE WEATHER AND ORDERED ME TO GIVE YOU A CRACK AT IT. GOOD LUCK. YOU'RE GOING TO NEED IT. THE FATE OF THOUSANDS OF PEOPLE IS IN YOUR HANDS!

Good grief. I had trouble deciding which shoes to wear. Edward was applying some pressure.

AND DON'T TELL ANYONE ABOUT ME OR OUR CONVERSA- TIONS. IF YOU DO, THE DEAL IS OFF. IF OPRAH OR THE SUPERMARKET TABLOIDS FIND OUT, THEY'LL MAKE A REAL MESS OF IT. BY THE WAY . . . WHAT DO YOU HAVE AGAINST MRS. BODECKER?

Nothing at all. It was the quilt.

WHAT QUILT?

Forget it.

DO YOU REALIZE SHE'S 93 YEARS OLD?

Yes. I hear that everywhere I go.

HMMM. YOU KNOW, UP HERE WE KEEP TRACK OF YOUR SINS, ERRORS AND MISCALCULATIONS, AND RIGHT NOW THIS BODECKER THING ISN'T LOOKING TOO GOOD ON YOUR RECORD.

I know. It won't happen again.

I attempted to print out the dialogue, but nothing appeared on the paper. A few moments later, the words disappeared from the screen. It was no use telling anyone about it because no one would believe me. I typed in a fore- cast for Saturday, calling for a high temperature of 80, and specifically stated that it would be sunny and 78 in Perrys- burg, where Mrs. Bodecker lived.

Everyone was so upset about Mrs. Bodecker's plight that I thought I'd better do something. I called a snow removal crew and told them to clear her drive, charging it to Pauley personally. After all, he started all the trouble by insisting I plug Mrs. Bodecker's quilt on the air.

9

Later, I was mulling the implications of my unorthodox pipeline to Heaven when the ringing of a telephone startled me.

"Jerry Sheldon? This is Luther Chambers!"

The name didn't ring any bells.

"I think you and I could make a lot of money," he said.

"I haven't got any money to invest in land deals, pig futures, or nursing home operations where residents are forced to live in squalor."

"Slow down, Jerry. You've got me wrong! I don't want any money from you. I want to make money for you! I'm an agent!"

Some television weathermen had agents, but I had never found one who wanted to handle me.

"To tell you the truth, Luther, I don't earn much. I can't afford to give you ten percent of my salary."

"Fifteen percent," he corrected.

"Well, I sure can't afford to give you fifteen percent. Besides, I've been doing some power negotiating with the station manager on my own. I don't need your services."

"Don't kid yourself. You may wangle yourself a piddling bonus or two, but to really capitalize on this weather thing, you need someone to manage you who knows the angles, someone who knows all about merchandising and spinoffs and tax loopholes, someone who can get you all the perks you deserve. I can show you how to make all the right moves."

I was wary. "How would I capitalize on 'this weather thing'?"

"Write a book. I'll sell it for big bucks, then we'll farm out the film rights! Go on a lecture tour! Market your own tee shirts! Frozen dinners! Fast food tie-ins! The sky's the limit!"

"I don't know, Luther. It sounds like you're just spittin' into the wind. How do I know you've got the clout and connections to do it?"

"Have you heard of Shaq O'Neal? Peyton Manning? Tiger Woods?"

"Sure."

"Of course you have! I can do the same for you!"

Later, I realized Luther never said he handled Shaq, Peyton or Tiger. He merely dropped their names into the conversation.

"Well, I *could* use the money," I conceded.

"Of course you could! Who couldn't? . . . Give me the go-ahead and I'll put things in motion. I'll send you a contract today. Just sign it and send it back. What do you say!"

"I suppose so . . ."

"All right! You won't be sorry, Jer! I'll be in touch!"

"But Luther . . . Luther!"

He had hung up.

So I had an agent.

Toledo's exclusive unseasonably hot weather led the "WWTT News at 6" again that night, with Eric's camera work graphically illustrating the difference between Toledo's tropical heat wave and the snowstorm in nearby Perrysburg.

After the video aired, Brent commented, "WELL, WE'RE CERTAINLY ENJOYING WONDERFUL WEATHER, BUT POOR MRS. BODECKER IS HAVING A ROUGH TIME OF IT. SHOULDN'T YOU DO SOMETHING TO HELP HER, JERRY . . . I MEAN, SINCE THIS SEEMS TO BE ALL YOUR FAULT?"

"LATE THIS AFTERNOON, I CALLED A SNOW REMOVAL COMPANY AND ASKED THEM TO CLEAR THE SNOW OFF THE SIDEWALKS, THE DRIVEWAY AND THE STREET IN FRONT OF MRS. BODECKER'S PROPERTY AT OUR EXPENSE."

"THAT'S GREAT," Fran commented.

Brent cleared his throat. "WELL, OUR HEARTS GO OUT TO YOU, MRS. BODECKER. IN OTHER NEWS TODAY . . ."

During the weather segment, I used my extra minute of airtime for an experiment: I attempted to create a small tornado in a "tornado tube". I'm sure I looked like a mad scientist as I cheerfully mixed a handful of esoteric ingredients together in an effort to create my own little twister.

Brent and Fran grew increasingly apprehensive.

"ARE YOU SURE THIS IS SAFE?" Brent asked.

"I THINK SO," I said, "BUT I'M NOT SURE. I'VE NEVER TRIED IT BEFORE."

"YOU'RE USING AN AWFULLY BIG TORNADO TUBE, AREN'T YOU?" Fran asked.

"IT WAS ALL I COULD FIND ON SHORT NOTICE," I explained. "OH, THERE IT IS. IT'S BEGINNING TO FORM NOW. SEE THAT SWIRLING MASS OF AIR! OUR OWN LITTLE TWISTER!"

About two seconds later, the twister broke through the tube and lurched toward the anchor desk, sending Brent's and Fran's scripts and notes flying across the newsroom before the tornado dissipated.

"NOW, LET'S LOOK AT THE WEATHER," I said. As I listed the

weather stats for Toledo, Brent and Fran could be heard in the background calling me filthy names.

After a commercial, I delivered the forecast I had prepared earlier on the computer.

"WE'RE IN FOR ANOTHER FINE DAY SATURDAY. MOSTLY SUNNY, WITH A FEW AFTERNOON CLOUDS. A HIGH OF 80. AND FOR PERRYSBURG AND MRS. BODECKER, IT WILL BE WARM, WITH SUNNY SKIES AND A HIGH OF 78." Music from *The Graduate* could be heard in the background as I said, "HERE'S TO YOU, MRS. BODECKER."

When the news staff gathered 'round to watch a tape of WORY's newscast, we were stunned. Dexter Bentley aired a telephone interview with Mrs. Bodecker. The situation at her home in Perrysburg had a different slant when she described it.

"SO WWTT—IN AN EFFORT TO MAKE UP FOR THE TERRIBLE THING THEY HAD DONE BY UNLEASHING A BLIZZARD ON YOU— SENT OVER A SNOW REMOVAL TRUCK THIS AFTERNOON. IS THAT RIGHT?" Dexter asked.

"THAT'S RIGHT."

"SO, NOW YOU CAN GET YOUR CAR OUT OF YOUR DRIVEWAY AND EVERYTHING IS ALL RIGHT?"

"WELL, IT WOULD HAVE BEEN, IF THE SNOW REMOVAL TRUCK HADN'T KNOCKED OVER A TREE IN MY FRONT YARD. THE TREE FELL ON THE POWER LINES GOING TO MY HOUSE AND KNOCKED OUT ALL MY ELECTRICITY."

"LET ME SEE IF I UNDERSTAND THIS," Dexter said. "YOU NOT ONLY HAVE A FOOT OF SNOW IN YOUR FRONT YARD, BUT YOU ARE NOW SITTING THERE IN THE DARK WITHOUT HEAT BECAUSE A SNOW REMOVAL TRUCK SENT OVER BY WWTT KNOCKED OUT YOUR POWER."

"THAT'S EXACTLY RIGHT," she noted. "THE POWER COMPANY SAYS ELECTRICITY WILL BE RESTORED SOMETIME NEXT WEEK."

"NEXT WEEK?" Dexter repeated, in amazement.

"YES. NEXT WEEK! IF I EVER GET MY HANDS ON THAT JERRY SHELDON, I'LL MURDER HIM! HE'S A MENACE!"

"HE CERTAINLY IS," Dexter agreed.

Fran, Brent, Morty and Pauley glared at me. "That poor old lady won't have any power till next week!" Fran noted, in case I missed it.

"I had nothing to do with the truck knocking out the power!" I insisted. I was getting a little tired of hearing about the Bodecker thing and my irritation boiled over. "And don't be sucked in by her 'harmless old lady' act. She's milking this for all it's worth, and she's loving every minute of it."

"That's a terrible thing to say!" Brent declared.

"You ought to be ashamed of yourself," Morty grumbled.

Morty was right, but I didn't worry any more about it because I was sure some government agency or charity would give old Mrs. Bodecker shelter and make sure she had food to eat.

A half hour before the late news aired Friday evening, Fran asked if I had plans for the weekend. "Are you taking Laura out?"

That's when it hit me. My workweek was ending. Saturday and Sunday were my days off, and Reggie Whelan would handle the weekend weather chores for WWTT. But I couldn't let that happen because Reggie, who didn't know the difference between a warm front and a hot water bottle, could really screw things up. He would use the official weather forecasts for Sunday and Monday, and Toledo would be thrown back into cold, wintry weather. Then, I'd be back on Monday, and we'd suddenly have beautiful weather again on Tuesday. The contrast would look highly suspicious.

Not only that . . . what if Reggie found messages from Edward on the weather computer? He wouldn't know what was going on. There was only course of action: I would need to handle the weekend weather chores, too. I had to get rid of Reggie for a few days.

I barged into Pauley Sherman's office.

"I need a favor," I said.

He glared at me. "You've got a lot of gall. What do you want now? My job?"

The thought had crossed my mind.

"You can't let Reggie do the weekend weather!"

Pauley was caught off-guard. "Why not? He's been doing it for four years."

"Reggie wouldn't know how to handle all this. He wouldn't understand what was going on. He would totally screw things up!"

"I think Brent and I had this conversation about you an hour ago."

"I'm serious, Pauley. If you like the way things are going—the beautiful weather, all the favorable publicity—you can't let Reggie do the weekend weather. *I* must do it."

"What am I supposed to tell Reggie? He's scheduled to work."

"Tell him there's a chili cookoff down in Texas you want him to cover."

"At the station's expense? You're out of your mind."

"Send him to New York. Tell him the network is interested in hiring him."

"Even Reggie isn't dumb enough to believe that."

"We've got to do something!" I insisted.

"All right. But he'd never fall for a chili cookoff or a network job interview." He picked up a brochure from his desktop. "The National Broadcasting Association is having its convention in New York City next week. J.P. wanted me to send someone to help the corporation set up and run its booth, but I couldn't spare anybody. I suppose we could send Reggie."

"Perfect!" I declared.

Pauley shook his head. "Not so fast. Let's think about this. Do we really want Reggie representing our station at the convention? Do we really want Reggie hanging out with J.P.? I mean, we're talking potential disaster, with the fallout threatening all of us."

"You're missing the big picture. They want to sell the station or close down our operation anyway. What difference does it make?"

"I suppose so. We're doomed either way. Right?"

"That's right!" I assured Pauley. "So get Reggie out of town fast. By tomorrow morning at the latest! I don't want him coming in to work tomorrow."

"All right. I'll take care of it. . . . You know, you've used up your favors for the next hundred and twenty years, Sheldon. When your star falls to earth and you're just doggie droppings on the floor like the rest of us, I'm going to own you lock, stock and barrel."

Obviously, Pauley had never talked to my new agent, Luther.

IV

PARADISE

10

The next morning, Reggie boarded a propjet bound for Cleveland—the first leg of his journey to New York City.

Toledo's heat wave continued to drive meteorologists and residents of nearby cities nuts. Tourists streamed into our tropical oasis from across the frigid Midwest. Their dollars jump-started the local economy. Motels, hotels and massage parlors were booked full.

As I escorted Laura and Kathy to Promenade Park early that afternoon, puffy cumulus clouds hovered overhead like UFOs searching for a landing site. Normally, the park was quiet and cold in early December, but on this warm and lusty day, it was crowded with fun-seekers clad in tee-shirts and shorts. When a teenager turned his radio up to "maximum eardrum damage" level, the park swayed to the beat of old Beach Boys hits. It was terrific. Instead of being held hostage by wintry weather, Toledo was pulsating and vibrant.

Laura threw a blanket on the ground and I stretched out beside her. We observed the human parade as it passed by.

"The things they're saying about you in the papers, Jerry—that you're into the occult, or that you're actually creating the weather. It all makes me very uneasy. You're fooling around with the natural order of things."

"I told you before . . . it's nothing. Sheer luck."

She grimaced. "You aren't leveling with me. This isn't coincidence or luck. There's got to be more to it, and whatever it is, you're at the center of it. I'm not buying your 'ah, shucks, it was just coincidence' act anymore."

"Why are you so suspicious? Relax and enjoy it." I gestured toward the people streaming into the park. "Look at them! They love it! It's like summer. Their juices are flowing, their hormones are raging. They're active and happy!"

"Jerry, don't talk about raging hormones when Kathy is around."

Kathy wandered over to play with another girl her age.

"What are you *doing* to make all this happen?" Laura asked.

"I can't tell you. I promised Edward I wouldn't tell anyone."

"Who's Edward?"

"That's one of the things I can't tell you. But I can assure you there's nothing illegal or sinister about it. It's all perfectly innocent! I simply forecast the weather and voilà, it comes true! Aside from God and possibly Irving Krick, I'm the most accurate weatherman in history!" Krick, who founded Strategic Weather Services, analyzed long-range weather patterns to devise accurate forecasts.

"If there's nothing wrong with what you're doing, why can't you tell me about it?"

"Good question. Edward is worried about what would happen if the tabloids and talk shows got ahold of it. They might take something wondrous and noble and turn it into dog food."

Laura rolled onto her side and looked deep into my eyes.

I hate it when women do that. It's like being given a lie detector test without your consent. One wrong word, one wrong flick of the eyelids, and you're dead meat.

"Believe me, Laura, I wouldn't have anything to do with this if it involved witchcraft, or devil's worship, or anything illegal. This is more like . . . well, magic!"

By suggesting it was magic I was dangerously close to Pauley Sherman's idea that this weather was a miracle. I had indeed fallen to new depths, but it was a little late to turn back.

"I don't believe in magic," Laura said.

"There's magic everywhere. Or miracles. Or wonderful coincidences. Call them what you wish. The film *It's a Wonderful Life*—that's magic. The high school basketball team from little Coldwater, Ohio, that played its way into the state finals a few years ago after winning only four of their twenty regular season games—that was magic. The way you and Kathy turn my dark days into glorious days—that's magic, too. Well, this weather is magic!"

Laura rolled over on her back and gazed at the heavens. "This weather is a little more than magic. It's incredible, when you consider that fifteen miles in any direction winter is in full swing."

"If the Disney Company did it, you'd think it was marvelous. You wouldn't doubt it for a minute. I do it, and you can't believe it."

"They have a few more billion dollars to work with than you do, Jerry."

"Not when I get done."

Laura eyed me suspiciously. "What are you talking about? Jerry Sheldon, are you trying to cash in on this 'magic'?"

I left Laura's question hanging without an answer. Kathy had finished playing, and it was time to go. But the real reason I avoided responding to Laura was that I could tell from the tone of the question that she would disapprove if I attempted to profit in any way from my weather prognostications. I, on the other hand, saw nothing wrong with writing a book about my life as a weatherman and selling the film rights, or marketing Toledo Weatherman tee shirts, or financing a line of Toledo Weatherman Frozen Macaroni Dinners. If Laura had married Bill Gates, there would be no Microsoft. He would not be a billionaire. She would tell him, "You can't profit off a computer operating system that you created because of your God-given talent!" If she had married Henry Ford, there would be no Ford Motor Company. "God gave you the idea, Henry. You can't commercialize it!"

So I tried to head off a confrontation over the marketing of the miracle by changing the subject.

"Are you ready for lunch, Pumpkin?" I asked Kathy.

"Sure."

We picked up our things and piled into the Buick for the short drive to Tony Packo's Cafe on Front Street.

Tony Packo's is a Toledo landmark, made even more famous by Toledo native Jamie Farr, who played Klinger on the "M*A*S*H" television series. The walls are lined with hot dog buns autographed by celebrities (a tradition started by Burt Reynolds). Specialties include Hungarian hot dogs and spicy chili.

Kathy led the way to a table as Laura admired the Tiffany lamps. We had barely started eating when Laura glared at me and growled, "Well?"

She has a knack for remembering exactly where a conversation left off fifteen or twenty minutes earlier. I, on the other hand, have trouble remembering what I was saying thirty seconds earlier. I could see trouble ahead if we got married. I'd never know what we were talking about. I'd be ready to start a new argument when I wasn't finished losing the previous one. I suspected Laura had purchased one of those "Improving Your Memory" video cassette packages that are advertised all night long on cable television. Memory training obviously would give a person an unfair advantage in domestic arguments, and I believe there should be legislation to protect the spouse in such situations. Something like the handgun legislation that requires a "cooling off" period before the gun is sold to the person. "I'm sorry, ma'am, but we can't sell you the memory package until we notify your spouse and determine if he wants to block the sale of such potentially dangerous information to you."

Well, I had done it again. During my daydreaming, I again lost contact with Laura.

"What did you say?" I asked her.

"I'm waiting for you to tell me you won't try to cash in on this magical weather of yours!"

"I wouldn't call it 'cashing in'. I thought I'd write a book, sell the rights to Hollywood, put out my own line of tee shirts, a few things like that. Luther says—"

"Luther? Who's Luther?"

"My agent."

"Your agent?" Laura was stunned.

"Well, yes. Luther normally handles big league jocks, but he was very interested. He seems to think I'm in the superstar class of weather forecasters."

"You can't cash in something like this, Jerry. You're the one who said it was 'magical'. Well, if it *is* magical, you don't sell out just because some turkeys are willing to pay for it."

"I suppose not. They wouldn't like it Up There."

I looked skyward.

"No, I don't think they would. The last I heard they thought some things were worth more than money. Jerry, don't let this go to your head! I wish you had never gotten involved in this. It makes me very nervous."

She took Kathy by the hand. They left Tony Packo's and hurried off down the street.

"Come back!" I pleaded. "Where are you going?"

Laura hurried on, pulling Kathy along. *"I need some space!"* she hollered, loud enough for my mother in Michigan to hear her. *"I need time to think. Before I marry Merlin the Magician, I've got to know what's going on!"*

That's the difference between men and women. Women want to know what's going on. Men don't care, as long as they have a television set, a cold beer and a warm woman. In that order.

"Let's talk about this!" I begged, but Laura and Kathy didn't look back.

I knew they wouldn't go far because I had the keys to the Buick in my pocket. That's when a bus came along, and they climbed aboard.

I walked slowly back to Tony Packo's, where I devoured another Hungarian hot dog while mulling things over. Fortunately, our little tiff hadn't affected my appetite.

11

At 6:30 the next morning, the ringing of the telephone shattered my slumber.

"I expect you to be over here at the usual time," the female voice said.

I was groggy and disoriented. "Of course. . . . Who is this?"

"It's Laura! You're taking Kathy and me to church!"

Although I usually escorted Laura and her daughter to church, I planned to sleep late on this particular Sabbath because I figured Laura would not be caught dead going anywhere with me after our confrontation the day before. I was wrong.

"I thought you were mad at me."

"I am, but we're going to church, Jerry Sheldon. You need all the divine guidance you can get!"

I also needed all the sleep I could get, but I thought it best not to mention that. "All right. I'll pick you up."

"And Jerry . . . you know that suit you wore to church last week . . . gray polyester with baggy pants? . . . Don't wear that. Give it to the Salvation Army, or Goodwill. It doesn't look good on you."

"That's my favorite suit!"

"Lose it, Jerry. It's vulgar and tacky. If you want to be a clown, join the circus. . . . Honey, I'm not nagging. I'm telling you this for your own good."

I thought that's what nagging was. I hung up the phone and trotted over to the back door, where I heaved my alarm clock as far as I could. I never did accept criticism gracefully, particularly early in the morning.

Hard Head McCullough, clad in red-and-white striped pajamas, opened a window.

"What the hell are you doing, Weatherman? What hit my house?"

"Must have been some of those huge birds that have been hanging around the neighborhood," I said. "The noise woke me up, too."

"Birds? Baloney!" He noticed remnants of the alarm clock scattered around his house and then spotted the dent the clock had made when it hit. *"You threw that at my house, didn't you, Weatherman! You're in trouble now. I'm like Israel. Whatever you do to me, you get back ten-fold. That wasn't a smart thing to do!"*

"I know," I said. "Now I've got to buy another alarm clock."

Hard Head slammed his window shut.

Forty minutes later, I climbed into my Buick and hightailed it over to Sylvania. It was unseasonably warm again—72 degrees, headed for a high of precisely 81. Light breezes blew in from the west at five to ten miles an hour.

"Hurry! We'll be late!" Laura shouted, as I drove up. She looked ravishing in a blue cotton dress with white trim. Kathy was a little doll in her red taffeta dress.

As they piled into the car, I grumbled something about churches that held services so early. After all, Sunday was supposed to be a day of rest.

"What did you say?" Laura asked.

"I said we're lucky that churches hold services so early." Kathy laughed.

"It's sweet of you to take us to church," Laura said, like I had a choice. If we married, I would be in for a lifetime of gentle but firm manipulation. But Laura was beautiful, and I decided I might as well accept her "guidance".

We soon arrived at the little white church on Sylvania Avenue. I have always been a sucker for stained glass windows and wooden pews, and the Fourth Baptist Church had them. Besides, the women of the church served up a terrific potluck dinner once a month. (I had learned several months earlier that the church frowned on those who showed up more often for the potluck dinners than they did for the worship services.)

The congregation numbered only about two hundred people, but that was fine with me because I preferred smaller churches. I never felt God and I had a close relationship in churches that seated a thousand people and looked more like auditoriums than places of worship. I never knew if I was waiting for a Toledo Walleye game or the Second Coming.

After parking in the paved lot adjoining the church, I escorted Laura and Kathy inside. Laura insisted we sit in pews near the front, "where the preacher can get a good look at us."

"That's why I prefer to sit in the back," I noted. She ignored me and led the way down the aisle.

As the organist ground out "How Great Thou Art", the Rev. Benjamin Throckmorton Furrow slumped in a chair behind the pulpit, seemingly lost in thought. He was a six-tyish, gray-haired, portly man, about five-foot-ten. He had come to the church after living a rowdy life, indulging in earthly pleasures. Now that he had been saved, he wanted to stop others from savoring those same earthly pleasures.

As I skimmed the church bulletin, I realized the service was built around a theme—Sinning Repairmen. My guess was that a repairman had ripped off Rev. Furrow by charging him sixty bucks an hour on a service call. But how did he find all those biblical verses and psalms pertaining to sinning repairmen?

After the sermon on "Greed and Selfishness as the Root of All Evil", Rev. Furrow located himself strategically at the exit as Laura, Kathy and I approached. He leaned down and whispered to me, "May I see you a minute, Jerry?"

We moved a few feet out of the path of foot traffic. "I didn't mean to snore during your sermon," I said. "I was tired. If your early service was held later—perhaps after the late service—people wouldn't be so apt to fall asleep during your sermons."

"Thank you for sharing that, Jerry, but you were the only one who was sleeping. That isn't what I wanted to talk to you about, although it would be nice if you could sleep on your time, not mine. . . . These strange stories that have been appearing in the newspapers . . . Is it true you can control the weather?"

I sighed. "So help me God, I haven't been doing anything evil or sinister with the weather. It's all on the up-and-up!"

"If you say there's nothing sinister or evil about your forecasts, I believe you."

He hesitated. I knew something was on his mind.

"Jerry, I was wondering about Saturday afternoon . . ."

"What about it?"

"The church is holding a potluck dinner, and because the weather has been so warm, I decided to hold it outdoors and make it a picnic. It would help if I could be sure the weather would be agreeable."

"This Saturday? Well, sure."

"Perhaps a high of 76 degrees. Just a few clouds drifting overhead."

"Well, yes, that could be arranged."

I sounded like a promoter fixing a fight.

We headed to the exit, where Laura and Kathy waited for us.

"Thank you, Jerry," Rev. Furrow said. "I knew you would come through."

"Nice doing business with you," I said.

He patted me on the shoulder. Was this the same minister who usually made me feel like a weed in the Garden of Eden because I dropped only a dollar bill in the collection plate?

As we walked to my car in the church parking lot, Laura cast a wicked glance my way.

"What did you do to Rev. Furrow?" she demanded. "Why is he acting like that?"

"Like what?"

"He was being nice to you. I want to know why!"

"He's a minister. That's his job."

"But he's never even talked to you before. He always had high standards. And what did you mean, 'nice doing business with you'?"

"He heard about my success with the weather and he asked me to do a little favor for him."

"You are disgusting, Jerry Sheldon. Corrupting our minister! Involving him in your shady schemes! Have you no shame?"

"Hold on! Don't jump to conclusions. I didn't corrupt Rev. Furrow. He weighed the evidence and concluded I'm not doing anything sinister with the weather. You should follow his lead, for he is a wise and moral man."

"Are there no depths to which you wouldn't stoop?"

I couldn't think of any, but I'm sure there were some. I never was much good at pop quizzes.

In the car, she resumed her attack on me. "So, what's this little favor the preacher asked you to do for him?"

"Nothing. It's trivial. Just forget it."

"What's the favor, Jerry?"

Laura was like a tiger. Once she got ahold of something, she wouldn't let go until it was torn to shreds.

"Nothing. Really! He wants me to arrange some nice weather for the church picnic on Saturday. That's all!"

"And you said you would do it?"

"What could I do? I was on the spot."

"You can't do that, Jerry! What's next? Charging corporations huge fees to give them the weather they want? . . . How about ten thousand dollars a day? Or, maybe twenty thousand?"

I considered dumping Luther and hiring Laura as my agent. Then I realized she was being sarcastic.

"Laura, I'm not going to sell my services. This weather forecasting gift I've been given is special. I wouldn't spoil it by setting a price on it."

"I should hope not!" she said.

Besides, I figured it was worth at least thirty grand a day.

12

The next afternoon, I was treated with new respect at WWTT because of the national news media's interest in me and Toledo's incredible weather. It was the first time someone working for our little one-horse station had messages on the "voice mail" answering system from "The CBS Evening News", the *Washington Post*, the Federal Trade Commission and the Weather Channel.

The *National Exposer*, a sleazy supermarket tabloid published in Florida, splashed a photo of Toledo's skyline across its front page under the headline

HOLY TOLEDO!
Weatherman Linked to Witchcraft

I suppose the demonic-looking face in the sun over Toledo was mine. Skimming the story inside, I discovered W.C. Muldoon and Dexter Bentley had told the *Exposer* I was a "pseudo-weatherman" who dabbled in weird things. That was the "link" to witchcraft.

For the first time in my life I received fan mail, as well as proposals of marriage from love-starved students at an all-female college in Massachusetts and an all-male college in Rhode Island. I also received a twenty-thousand-dollar check in the mail. All I had to do to earn the money was to heat up Nome, Alaska's climate about fifty degrees. I sent the check back and suggested the letter writer use the money to move to southern California.

Surrounded by fan mail, I realized Brent and the others had been wrong. I was not merely a weatherman at a little shack of a television station in Toledo. People across the country and around the world had heard of me and Toledo's Miracle Weather. I was well on my way to doing something special with my life.

I was still opening letters when Daisy Edwards, an editor with *Weatherwise* magazine, called.

"We have been reading about Toledo's fantastic weather, Jerry, and we would like to do a cover story on you."

Me—on the cover of *Weatherwise*? I was ecstatic. You could offer me the covers of *Time* and *Newsweek*, give me the starring role in a film, find a doctor who could actually cure the common cold—none of it could compare with having my mugshot on the cover of *Weatherwise*. It just doesn't get any better than that. But I didn't want to appear too eager.

"Well, sure," I told Daisy. "I'll see if I can work you into my schedule."

"If it's that much trouble, forget it," Daisy grumbled.

"No, wait! I was joking! Any time is fine. We can do it now. . . . Hello? . . . Hello? . . ."

The editor had hung up. I learned a valuable lesson: if Fate comes calling, don't play hard to get.

In mid-afternoon, I was creating a computer sequence show-ing a cold front swooping down over the Rocky Mountains when Pauley slithered into my weather cubicle.

"I just got a call from J.P. He's got a new drinking buddy."

"How nice for J.P.," I said. I couldn't understand why Pauley wasted my time with such trivia.

"His new drinking buddy is Reggie . . . and Reggie is telling him all about our operations."

"He doesn't know anything about our operations," I pointed out.

"Exactly. But he's been amusing J.P. with a few anecdotes—such as the time I threw a smoldering cigarette into a wastebasket, starting a three-alarm fire. And how I told the staff J.P. had taken over a perfectly healthy television station in Tucson and run it into the ground. That little bugger is dangerous!"

"J.P.?"

"No! Reggie! J.P. heard about what's happening to the weather here and he figured it was great. It would boost our ratings, draw attention to the station and allow him to raise advertising rates. Then his new buddy Reggie convinced J.P. he was wrong—Reggie said the weather gimmick would boost ratings in the short-run, but as soon as the miracle weather ended we'd be in last place again. So, thanks to Reggie, J.P. is on my case again, saying we've got to make substantial changes or when the ratings plummet, he's going to fire us all, put Reggie in charge of the station and air reruns of 'Beavis and Butthead' and 'My Mother the Car'."

"It wasn't very smart of you to send Reggie to help J.P. at the convention," I suggested.

Pauley glared at me. "I never thought he'd cozy up to J.P. I wouldn't have sent him anywhere if it weren't for you. This is all *your* fault, Sheldon."

"Don't blame me. I wanted to send Reggie to a chili cookoff. He couldn't cause any trouble there."

Pauley was on the verge of losing his temper. "The station couldn't afford to send Reggie to the suburbs, much less Texas. I was able to get him out of town because I'm billing corporate headquarters for Reggie's trip to the convention!"

"Good grief," I said. "If J.P. finds out about that, you'll really be in trouble." I reached for the phone. "Audrey, get me J.P.'s office in New York."

Pauley snatched the receiver from me and placed it back on the mount. "Why don't you use some of that humor in your weather segments?"

"I thought I did."

"Well, let's round up the news crew. I've got to turn things around immediately! . . . Do you think I could get away with firing Reggie?"

"It's not smart to fire the boss' drinking buddy," I pointed out.

Pauley pleaded his case for a new, improved Happy Talk as Brent picked his nose and Fran, Morty, Harry and I played a hand of poker.

"The pressure is on, boys and girls. J.P. wants immediate results. The senile old goat hasn't produced a newscast in thirty years, but he considers himself qualified to rip ours to pieces. He says our broadcasts lack professionalism—"

"Pair of aces," Fran told Morty. "What have you got?"

"Two pair."

"Cheater," Fran grumbled.

"—and excitement! There's no shock value! No momentum that keeps the news moving along, and no rapport with the viewers."

Brent shook his head. "And that comes from an old duffer who can't flush a toilet without help."

"Yes," Pauley said, *"but he's the boss, and his word is Law. Now, I think I've figured out why the Happy Talk isn't working."*

"Because it's a frivolous, idiotic concept?" Harry guessed.

"No. It's the image each of you projects on the tube. You don't come across as decent, average people—the kind viewers identify with."

"Two aces," said Fran, laying them on the table.

"Three aces," Morty countered.

"All right. Who tampered with the cards?" I demanded.

"Polls show the audience doesn't empathize with you," Pauley insisted. *"They don't like you very much!"*

"Who cares whether they like us?" Harry growled. "I thought we were supposed to give them the news and then get out of their living rooms."

"But if they don't like you, they won't watch you at all! You can't give them the news if they're watching another channel! You need the common touch, like the guy next door, or the friendly supermarket checkout girl."

"Or the friendly neighborhood axe murderer," suggested Harry.

"You've got to be more likable. You need to talk the language of ordinary people. Reach out and touch a responsive chord in them. You can do that, can't you?"

Harry shook his head. "You're such a jerk, Pauley. It's the news that matters—"

"—and the weather!—" I interjected.

"—not our personalities."

"Get real," Pauley said. *"This is a new century! It's the medium, not the message, that counts! It's all form, all image and hype. Nobody cares about substance anymore!"*

"I know my mother doesn't," Brent noted.

"There!" Pauley said, relieved someone finally agreed with him. *"You see!"*

"My mother's in a psycho ward at the hospital," Brent said. "She doesn't care much about anything."

When I summoned Edward to transmit Tuesday's forecast, he chided me . . .

> ISN'T THE FORECAST YOU COOKED UP FOR TUESDAY THE SAME AS TODAY'S?
>
> No, Edward. Today, the high will be 82. Tomorrow's high will be 81.
>
> HEAVENS! HOW COULD I BE SO WRONG?

I suspected Edward was being sarcastic, but I wasn't sure. I didn't think spiritual entities were supposed to be sarcastic.

> YOU'RE IN A RUT, JERRY. HOW ABOUT SHOWING MORE IMAGINATION? HOW ABOUT SHOWING SOME GUTS? WOULD YOU LIKE TO GIVE TOMORROW'S WEATHER ANOTHER SHOT?

To please Edward, I revised the forecast:

> All right. Here goes ... Mostly sunny tomorrow. A few clouds in the morning. High 78.
>
> WOW. TIME TO GET OUT THE OLD FUR COATS.

I wondered if I could ask to be assigned to some other contact in Heaven, one who wasn't so uppity.

I finally realized what Edward was trying to tell me. My forecasts had been rather dull. And it wasn't like me. Two months earlier, I had been broadcasting from the middle of a hurricane. Eight months before that, I parachuted out of a plane to give viewers a close-up look at clouds. The weather had been so sublime the last few days that I forecast more sunny days automatically, without giving it much thought.

It was time to be more daring and adventurous, but without risking my popularity. (People seemed to love the summer-like weather I had created.) I overhauled Tuesday's forecast one more time . . .

```
Partly cloudy and breezy. High of 75.
```

Edward's reaction was brief . . .

```
YOU HAVE LED A VERY SHELTERED LIFE, JER.
```

The news staff took Pauley's pleadings about developing the common touch to heart. That night the "News at 6" seemed more like "The Wild, Wacky, Wonderful News at 6". As we went on the air, cameras revealed the news crew's new look. Brent Sanders was decked out in a Gandhi jacket . . . Fran Rosen in a punk hairdo and tight-fitting blouse . . . Morty in a black leather jacket and pearl earrings . . . and I was wearing a plaid shirt and farmer's overalls. Harry, uncompromising as always, settled for a suit and tie.

Pauley had been tied up on a phone call to J.P. and didn't see the news crew's new look until twenty seconds before air time.

"What is this? 'Ma and Pa Kettle and Hell's Angels Give the News'?"

"You wanted us to appeal to the common folk," Morty reminded him.

"Well, sure, but I was talking about the way you act, and what you say. I didn't mean for you to drag out your old Halloween costumes. Besides, I was thinking more of ordinary city dwellers."

"You have a lot of trouble making up your mind," Brent grumbled. "I'll give you the name of my mom's shrink."

"Three seconds," director Barb Farley announced.

As Pauley hastily retreated to the Control Room, Brent described for viewers Toledo's latest installment of incredible weather.

"WELL, DUDES, HERE WE ARE IN DAY FIVE OF THIS WEATHER THING, AND WE ARE GETTIN' HIGH ON SUN. WE ARE IN THE EYE OF THE HURRICANE, THE MOUTH OF THE VOLCANO. THE ENTIRE NATION IS WATCHIN' US. I GUESS THEY'VE GOT NOTHIN' BETTER TO DO. BUT WHAT IS IT THEY'RE WATCHING? THIS—"

Film that Eric shot around the city and at the lakefront rolled.

"THEY'RE WATCHING US DO THE BEACH BOYS BIT IN DECEMBER, WHILE A FEW MILES AWAY WINTER ROARS ALONG IN FULL STEAM. THEY'RE WATCHING OUR WEATHERMAN, JERRY SHELDON, WHO SEEMS TO HAVE SOME SORT OF MYSTERIOUS POWER, BECAUSE HE'S THE ONE WHO HAS BEEN SETTIN' UP THIS AWESOME WEATHER. THEY'RE WATCHING US TO SEE IF THIS WEATHER THING IS SOMETHING THEY CAN STEAL AND USE FOR THEIR OWN GREEDY MOTIVES. SO, TOLEDO IS WHERE IT'S AT, MAN, AND WE'D BETTER ENJOY OUR MOMENT IN THE SUN, BECAUSE WHO KNOWS WHEN THIS FANTASTIC RIDE WILL END AND WE'LL ALL BE WALLOWING IN SLUSH, SLEET AND SNOW, LIKE OUR POOR, UNFORTUNATE NEIGHBORS. FOR NOW, HOWEVER, WE CAN STICK UP OUR NOSES AT OUR NEIGHBORS AND SAY . . . 'SCREW YOU, JERKS' . . ."

"Oh, God," we could hear Pauley moaning through our earphones.

From there, the quality of the newscast slid downhill. Finally, it was time for my weather segment.

"WHAT'S UP WITH THE WEATHER, JER?" said Brent. "YOU RECKON TOMORROW WILL BE ANOTHER HOT ONE?"

I donned a straw hat and flicked a wad of pink hair from Fran's wig off my overalls. "I'D BET MY TRACTOR ON IT. BUT OUT WEST, ALL SORTS OF HEAVY DUTY STORM ACTION IS MESSING UP THE WEATHER PICTURE. ALTHOUGH ALL THAT ROTTEN WEATHER WILL

BE SWEEPING INTO OHIO A FEW DAYS FROM NOW, TOLEDO WILL BE SPARED."

On the blue screen behind me, viewers could see a pot-belly stove.

"NOW, PULL UP A CHAIR AROUND THE OLD STOVE AND I'LL TELL Y'ALL, NEIGHBOR TO NEIGHBOR, ALL ABOUT WHAT'S HAPPENING WITH THE WEATHER IN TOLEDO."

After muddling through the weather stats for the day, I delivered the forecast.

I planned to stop by Laura's after work, but when I called, she said she was too tired, she had a headache, and she had to get up early in the morning. I expected one excuse but not all three. I got the definite impression she was still upset about my weather deal with Rev. Furrow and didn't want to see me. I drove home instead and eyeballed a Weather Channel documentary about droughts in East Africa.

13

Television stations in major markets receive Nielsen ratings overnight and weekly. In smaller markets like Toledo, however, ratings are distributed only four times a year. WWTT's ratings for November had not included our Miracle Weather Forecasts, so ordinarily we would wait months for the next ratings. However, because J.P. Bengolo had hired a firm—Bird, Bird, Burgett and Bird—to conduct an extensive telephone survey of television viewers in Toledo, we were anxious to see what these unofficial ratings showed.

Tuesday, we received the news. We had jumped to third place in evening news in the Toledo market because of our strong showing during the weather segment. Bird, etc. said we would have had a higher rating if more people had stuck around to hear the rest of our newscast. Nevertheless, the third-place ranking excited all of us—especially Pauley.

With the "miracle weather" in high gear, Luther Chambers exploited it from every possible angle. He focused on merchandising tie-ins and movie-of-the-week offers, but when I told him about the ratings, he decided to drop by Pauley's office immediately for a little power negotiating on my behalf. Who knew when my bubble would burst? As Luther put it, "today's top sirloin is tomorrow's chopped hamburger". Pithy little sayings like that made me think my agent saw me as nothing more than a side of beef to be slaughtered and sold to the highest bidder.

When Audrey, our receptionist/office girl, ushered Luther and me into Pauley's office, Luther shook hands with Pauley warmly.

"Nice to meet you, Pauley," Luther boomed. "I want you to know that I appreciate your sense of humor."

"What do you mean?" Pauley asked warily.

"When Jerry told me what you were paying him, I had a good laugh. I thought he was joking. You must have been a slave owner in another life. But I don't blame you. You're in a dog-eat-dog business, and people who run businesses do whatever they can get away with."

"Actually, I've always believed that everyone in our newsroom is *overpaid*," Pauley asserted.

"You're probably right," Luther agreed sympathetically.

I was aghast.

"That's why we've got plenty of room for negotiating," Luther continued. "You can chop some of the excess out of the other newsroom salaries so you can give our boy here what he's worth."

Brent, Fran, Morty, Harry and Eric would love that idea. I would be as popular in the newsroom as Dracula on date night. Maybe it would be better to take the excess out of Pauley's salary.

Luther rambled on: "Let's not waste time shadow boxing, Pauley. You've seen the ratings. You've seen the publicity. You know that Jerry here is the best thing that's happened to this station since you dumped your black-and-white equipment and switched to color broadcasting."

Actually, WWTT didn't invest in color broadcasting equipment until 1991. J.P. said he wanted to be sure all the bugs had been worked out of it.

"Your newscasts were dead last in the market. Last week—thanks to my boy here, and him alone—you were Number Three!"

"Yes, we should all have a beer together sometime to celebrate it," Pauley said. "Well, if that's all, I have another appointment in five minutes, and—"

"Then I'll get to the point," Luther said. "Jerry should be richly rewarded for what he's doing for you and the station. I tell you what . . . just give us the station and we'll be happy."

Pauley wasn't sure if Luther was joking. I wasn't either. I didn't *want* the station. As soon as my forecasting powers waned, the station would teeter on the brink of bankruptcy again.

"You have a well-developed sense of humor, too," Pauley noted.

"I'm glad we get along so well," Luther said. "I'm sure we can quickly come to terms on a few items I wanted to bring up."

He pulled out of his briefcase a stack of papers the size of the King James version of the Bible.

"First, Jerry's salary. Now, Jerry's salary is ridiculously low. Minimum wage—"

"Jerry earns a lot more than minimum wage," Pauley pointed out.

"Minimum wage *for television weathermen*," Luther said. He plopped part of the papers on Pauley's desk. "Our survey of salaries in the top three hundred markets in the country shows that Jerry ranks the lowest among weathercasters! Now, are we going to quit wasting time and talk serious money, or should I take my client to another station and leave you and your station in the dust?"

Pauley sighed. "How much do you want?"

"Seventy grand will do for starters."

Pauley's eyes opened wide. "That's twenty grand more than I make! You've got to remember, Luther, this is a television station on the verge of bankruptcy, not the Chase Manhattan Bank!"

Luther pulled a small cassette recorder out of his pocket and pushed the play button. One of the new station breaks Pauley had just begun airing, complete with music, could be heard:

"You're watching WWTT—Toledo's Miracle Weather Station!"

Pauley sighed. "Forty grand."

"Can't hear you," Luther grumbled.

"He said 'forty grand'," I told Luther, trying to be helpful.

"Leave this to me," he growled. He turned to Pauley again. "Sixty-nine grand."

"Fifty," Pauley said.

"Can't hear you," Luther said. He played the station break again.

"You could hear me if you'd turn off the damn recording," Pauley grumbled. "Fifty-five."

"Still can't hear you." Luther played the promo again.

Pauley shifted uneasily in his chair. I could tell he wanted to get this torture over with. "Sixty. That's my last offer."

"I'm willing to compromise," Luther declared. "Sixty-eight."

"I've come up from forty grand to sixty," Pauley pointed

out. "You've come down from seventy to sixty-eight. That isn't what I call compromising."

"Sixty-seven, and that's my final offer," Luther said.

"All right," Pauley grumbled.

I was beginning to think I had signed up with the right agent.

"Now for item Number Two," Luther said. "Jerry is working out of a weather room that's smaller than the john in my house. He wants a weather room that's three times larger!"

"What? I'd be forced to give him my office!" Pauley screamed.

"All right, if you insist," Luther said. "Next item—"

"Hold on!" Pauley bellowed. "I didn't agree to do it. I merely said if he wanted an office that big, he'd have to take mine."

"And I accepted," Luther noted.

"Let's compromise on this," Pauley said. "He can work out of the john in your house."

"Love your sense of humor, Pauley, but your first offer was better. He'll take your office. Next item—"

In the next ten minutes, Pauley agreed to sign up with a private weather forecasting operation, purchase additional forecasting equipment and give me a subscription to *Hurricane Trackers* magazine.

Luther's negotiating prowess awed me, but I never had the guts to take over Pauley's office. I heard rumors he had booby-trapped it.

Tuesday afternoon was warm and pleasant, but the "light winds" I had forecast turned out to be blustery gales, reaching thirty-five miles per hour, with gusts to seventy. Reports of wind damage flowed into the WWTT newsroom from throughout the city. WORY's broadcasting tower toppled, forcing the station—and Dexter's weathercast—off the air. A dozen homeowners and WORY's owners called, threatening to sue the station. It was much more than I had bargained for. I fired up the Cloudchaser computer and asked Edward what had gone wrong.

> I suppose I didn't communicate with you clearly. I called for light winds, not another Hurricane Helga.
> YOU ASKED FOR A "PARTLY CLOUDY AND BREEZY" DAY. ON THE BEAUFORT SCALE, WINDS CAN BE ANYTHING FROM 1 MPH TO 300 MPH OR MORE. YOU SHOULD BE MORE SPECIFIC.
> Use a little common sense, Edward. If I ask for a breeze, that's what I expect. If I want a damn hurricane, I'll call for one.
> I HATE DEALING WITH AMATEURS.

I worded my forecast for the next day very carefully, scheduling sunny weather with a high of 77.

I had been wondering about the limits of my forecasting powers. Could I control the weather for Cleveland . . . or Chicago . . . or perhaps even New York? Why not the whole country, or the world?

> Hold on, Edward. I'm not done yet.
> WHAT DO YOU MEAN? YOU SENT THE FORECAST. QUIT BUGGING ME.
> There's more . . . In Detroit, it will be sunny tomorrow, with a high of 78.
> DETROIT?
> And Cincinnati will be mild, with a high of 72.
> WHAT DO YOU THINK YOU'RE DOING? YOU'VE GOT NOTHING TO DO WITH THE WEATHER IN DETROIT AND CINCINNATI!

Can I forecast for any place else besides Toledo?

YOU HAVE TROUBLE HANDLING TOLEDO'S WEATHER. WHY DO YOU WANT TO MESS WITH THE WEATHER ELSE-WHERE?

Man's unceasing desire to explore and learn.

FORGET IT. YOU'VE GOT THE TOLEDO FRANCHISE--FOR THE TIME BEING, ANYWAY--AND THAT'S ALL. QUIT TRYING TO GET MY JOB. YOU REALLY ARE A GREEDY LITTLE BUGGER, AREN'T YOU.

Well, it was worth a try.

Have you given any other forecasters the type of powers you've given me?

ABOUT SIXTY YEARS AGO, A WEATHERMAN IN SEATTLE WAS RIDICULED FOR PREDICTING FEROCIOUS THUN-DERSTORMS ON A DAY THAT TURNED OUT TO BE SUNNY. NOT A CLOUD IN THE SKY. I FELT SORRY FOR HIM, SO I GAVE HIM CONTROL OF THE WEATHER IN WESTERN WASHINGTON.

What happened?

IT'S BEEN RAINING THERE EVER SINCE. THE RAIN FOREST NEAR SEATTLE SOMETIMES RECEIVES OVER 400 INCHES OF RAIN A YEAR.

I've heard that.

WELL, IT WAS DESERT LAND BEFORE THE KID GOT HOLD OF IT. HE WAS A LOT LIKE YOU.

Why didn't you take back control of the weather when rain continued to fall?

I WAS NEW AT THIS. INSTEAD OF GIVING HIM CONTROL ON A TRIAL BASIS--LIKE I GAVE YOU--I GAVE HIM TOTAL CONTROL. HE WOULDN'T GIVE IT BACK.

I tried to find out more about Edward. He mentioned he had lived in Chicago in the middle of the nineteenth century.

Did you forecast weather in Chicago?

NO. I DELIVERED COAL.

Why were you put in charge of the weather if you don't have experience as a meteorologist?

I LEARN FAST.

I'm beginning to understand why the weather on this planet is so screwed up.

AND I'M BEGINNING TO UNDERSTAND WHY YOU WORK FOR A FIFTH-RATE STATION IN TOLEDO.

I didn't think they let cranky people in Heaven. Aren't you supposed to be nicer?

YOU SHOULD HAVE SEEN ME WHEN I DELIVERED COAL. I'M MUCH NICER NOW.

14

WEDNESDAY, DECEMBER 10

Over at WORY, Dexter Bentley was so jealous of the publicity I was receiving that he couldn't stand it. The high winds that knocked Dexter off the air didn't endear me to him, either. Some of our buddies in the WORY newsroom told us Dexter spent hours each day plotting my downfall. After all, he had handled weather forecasts for Toledo radio and television stations since shortly after World War II. When I started doing amazing things with the weather and grabbing the headlines, Dexter found himself playing second fiddle. He couldn't accept that without a fight.

Brent Lassiter and Dexter occasionally crossed paths on their late night carousing at local nightspots and they often had a drink together. Brent told me on Wednesday that he had run into Dexter at the Kitty Kat Club the previous evening. As the liquor flowed, Brent and Dexter became more convivial. Dexter pressed Brent to reveal the secret of my forecasting success.

"I told him I didn't know what you were doing to the weather, but he wasn't satisfied. He pestered me about your work habits, and what happened the night of the accident.

About two in the morning, Dex concluded your weather computer had something to do with it."

I shrugged. "Well, if you see him again, tell him he was on the right track with the ozone layer."

Later that afternoon, I headed for my weather cubicle to fire up the magical Cloudchaser computer.

I stopped dead in my tracks. The contraption on my desk was not my magical weather computer. It was a new one. Bigger, shinier, more expensive. The logo on the front of the machine identified it as a Colorglow 36L. The old Cloudchaser computer was nowhere in sight.

"Get Pauley Sherman!" I ordered Audrey. "I want to see him now!"

About two minutes later Audrey returned with the station manager in tow.

"Where's my computer, Pauley?"

"It's gone, Jerry. I got you a new one. It cost a small fortune, but what the hell—you're worth it to the station, and I want to keep you happy."

"I'm not happy, Pauley! Do I look happy?"

He studied me closely. "No. And I'm not sure why ... You and that bully of an agent you hired have been complaining you need more equipment, more space, links to private forecasting services ..."

"But we never said anything about getting rid of my old computer. I need the Cloudchaser! Get it back!"

"I don't think we can do that, Jer. The store gave me a discount because I traded in the Cloudchaser for the new one. They're going to junk the Cloudchaser and use the parts. This is much more powerful. It's got so much memory you could put all the weather data on the hard drive and still have space left for the text of all the books in the Toledo library."

"Pauley . . ."

"All right. So it's not a big library. Tell me what you want."

"I want my computer back. Immediately! You have no idea what you're messing with here."

"It just isn't possible, Jer."

"Which computer store took it?"

"The User Friendly Shop. On Sixth Street."

I grabbed my coat, ran out of the newsroom and was still running when I hit the street. I hopped into my Buick and sped through two red traffic lights on the way to Sixth Street.

After parking in a no-parking zone, I hustled inside the User Friendly Shop. It was about the size of a convenience store. Computers of various shapes and sizes squatted on desks scattered throughout the store. The walls held shelves filled with computer software. At the far end of the store was a counter manned by a nerdy-looking middle-aged man in a wrinkled blue suit. I marched back to the counter.

"I want my computer!" I demanded, breathlessly.

The salesman smiled. "That's what we like to hear. What can I sell you today, sir?"

I grabbed him by the lapels of his suitcoat and shook him till his false teeth rattled. "Nothing, you imbecile! Someone from this shop stole my computer!"

"You must be mistaken. We don't deal in hot merchandise. We are completely legit."

He wasn't getting the message. I shook him a few more times. "My weather computer! My boss gave you my old

Cloudchaser when he bought a new computer from you. I want the old one back!"

"Oh, that old thing. Why would you want it? It looked like it had been thrown into an oven. Our new Colorglow 36L is much faster, and it's got a massive hard drive—enough storage to hold all your weather data and have enough room left for—"

"I know. Enough room left for all the books in the Toledo library. I don't *want* the Toledo library on my hard drive. I want my Cloudchaser back. It's a very special computer. If you touch even one chip on its circuit boards—"

I heard another salesman comment, "Some jerks really get attached to their computers."

The salesman I roughed up pushed my hands away from his suitcoat. "If you'll try to remain calm, I'll see if I can find it for you."

He disappeared into the back room. A few moments later, he returned carrying a broken keyboard.

"Sorry, sir. This seems to be all that's left of it."

"Oh, no!" I wailed.

Just then, a repairman burst out of the back room. "Al, I was thinkin' of the wrong computer. Here it is."

He was carrying my Cloudchaser, and it seemed to be intact.

"That's it!" I shouted, and I grabbed it out of his hands.

"Not so fast," the salesman said. "We took this in trade. If you want it back, you'll have to pay eight hundred more for your new Colorglow workstation."

"I don't want the new computer. I'm giving it back to you! Give Pauley Sherman his money back, and we'll call it even."

"Well, I don't know," the salesman said. "Seems like we ought to get something out of this for our trouble."

I put the computer on the counter, grabbed the salesman by the lapels again and started shaking him.

"All right, all right! Just take your computer and get out of here!"

When I returned to the weather cubicle, the new Colorglow 36L was gone. I assumed Pauley had finally gotten the message and taken it back to the shop. I was hooking up the old Cloudchaser when Pauley wandered into my office.

"I don't know why you want that old thing when you can have a new computer," he grumbled. "What did you do with the Colorglow?"

"I didn't do anything with it. I thought you took it."

"I didn't take it. Quit kidding around. It's an eight-thousand dollar machine. You didn't throw it out the window, did you?"

"I told you, Pauley. I didn't touch it. It was here when I left. Maybe the computer shop sent somebody over to pick it up."

Pauley called the User Friendly Shop. They weren't very friendly, Pauley said, and they had not picked up the computer.

"Good Lord! It's been stolen!" he exclaimed.

"Don't be silly," I said. "No one would just walk right in here and steal a computer."

Pauley questioned the newsroom crew. Fran said she noticed a man dressed like a computer repairman carrying the ColorGlow out of the newsroom.

"What did he look like?"

"I didn't pay much attention. He wore glasses and had a funny-looking, bushy mustache. I can't put my finger on it, but there was something familiar about him."

Pauley reported the computer theft to police. I thought no
more about it. I was happy to have the old one back. When
I fired up the Cloudchaser on Wednesday afternoon, a message from Edward appeared on the screen.

```
JERRY?  OH,  JERRRRRRRRYYY!!!  ARE  YOU  THERE,
JERRY?
```

 I sat down and typed . . .

```
I'm here.
THANK HEAVENS. TWO HOURS AGO I TRIED TO REACH
YOU AND I FOUND MYSELF TALKING TO A REPAIRMAN
AT SOMETHING CALLED THE USER FRIENDLY SHOP.
WHAT IN THE WORLD IS THE USER FRIENDLY SHOP?
It's a store where they sell computers.
OH. THAT EXPLAINS IT. HE ASKED ME IF I HAD A LOT
OF MEMORY. I SAID I COULD REMEMBER THINGS FROM
TWO CENTURIES AGO. I GUESS THAT CONFUSED HIM.
```

Preoccupied and stressed out, I quickly typed an innocuous
forecast calling for mild weather on Thursday and a high of
65. Recalling Edward's comments about my timid forecasting, I decided to add an extra touch—a little morning fog.

That Wednesday evening, strange things began happening
over at WORY. Dexter's forecast was even weirder and farther removed from reality than usual. After our newscast
ended, our crew viewed a videotape of Dexter's performance. We were stunned.

"TONIGHT, THE WEATHER IN TOLEDO IS TAKING A NEW COURSE,"
Dexter declared. "FROM NOW ON, WORY IS THE ONLY STATION IN
TOWN THAT CAN PROVIDE YOU WITH DETAILED, ACCURATE FORECASTS.
THANKS TO BREAKTHROUGH TECHNOLOGY, WE CAN PROVIDE YOU WITH
FORECASTS UNEQUALED ANYWHERE ELSE. SO LET'S GET DOWN TO BUSI-

NESS. TONIGHT, WE'LL HAVE CLOUDY SKIES AND A LOW OF 39. THURS-
DAY, LOOK FOR SUNNY SKIES AND A HIGH OF 54—EXCEPT OVER AT
JERRY SHELDON'S HOUSE, WHERE HUNDRED-MILE-AN-HOUR WINDS AND
THUNDERSTORMS WILL MOVE IN."

"My house? What's he trying to pull?"

"Maybe he's on the same wavelength to the Twilight
Zone that you are," Morty suggested.

"That isn't possible. I've got an exclusive deal. This terri-
tory is assigned to me."

"Could be that he's drinking more than usual," Fran suggested.

"That isn't possible, either," Dexter's drinking buddy,
Brent, said. "He'd be dead."

THURSDAY, DECEMBER 11

The next day, the temperature reached 65 throughout the
city, including my neighborhood. I had hit the forecast on
the nose. The fog which I had thrown in as an afterthought
turned out to be disastrous, however. Low visibility caused
thirteen crashes, including a five-car pileup on Interstate 475
that injured three Toledoans. The fog also grounded air traffic for two hours at Toledo Express Airport, where a propjet
coming in from Cleveland narrowly missed slamming into
the terminal building. These mishaps inspired more complaints and a reprimand from Pauley, who ordered me to
"knock off the fancy stuff".

I was caught in the middle. When I issued timid forecasts,
Edward complained. When I tried to be a little adventurous,
Edward got carried away and half of Toledo complained. I
decided to back off from the adventurous stuff until I could
figure things out. I issued a pleasant but harmless forecast
for Friday.

Dexter's forecast for Thursday had been far off the mark, as usual. His "breakthrough technology" failed dismally. I concluded that job stress and unbounded envy over my success in forecasting Toledo's weather had been too much for him.

Yet, Dexter seemed determined to push the situation even farther. He declared that Friday would be rainy throughout the city, with highs in the upper 60s—except over at my house, where "hurricane-force winds" would batter me.

FRIDAY, DECEMBER 12

The following day, it was 82 and sunny throughout the city, just as I had forecast, but I was getting a little ticked off at Dexter for singling me out as a target for wicked weather. Nevertheless, the knowledge that Dexter was making an even bigger jackass of himself than usual comforted me.

That afternoon, Morty called Larry Bacon, the sports anchor at WORY, to discuss an upcoming charity basketball game involving "sports personalities" from Toledo. During the course of the conversation, he asked Larry what Dexter's problem was. Bacon said that since Dexter had switched to a new weather computer earlier in the week, his forecasts had been weirder than usual.

When Morty told the rest of the newsroom crew what Bacon had said, Fran reminded us of Brent's run-in with Dexter, when Dexter concluded my weather computer had to be the key to the fantastic weather we were having.

"Good Lord," I said. "Dexter stole our weather computer! He thought that if he had our computer, his forecasts would automatically come true!"

Old Dexter was on the right track, of course, but he had stolen the wrong weather computer—he got the new Colorglow that Pauley had tried to force on me!

"Why, that old thief," Morty said. "We ought to call the police and turn him in. It would serve Dexter right!"

I suggested a different course of action.

Fran placed a call, all right, but she called the WORY offices, not the police. She told the receptionist to inform their "crazy old weatherman" that police would be tipped off the next day where they could find the WWTT weather computer, and that Dexter should prepare for a long stay at a state penitentiary.

Then we set up some cameras and waited as we went about our business of preparing for the evening newscast.

A few minutes after four on Friday afternoon, a chubby old bespectacled repairman with a goofy-looking mustache wandered into our newsroom carrying a Colorglow 36L computer. He glanced furtively from side-to-side as he moved closer to my weather room. I watched the whole thing from the anchor desk, where Brent, Fran and I had been discussing the evening newscast.

Once inside the weather room, the repairman placed the computer on the desk and immediately left, hurrying toward the newsroom exit while trying to look nonchalant. I hollered at him.

"Dexter, you old reprobate. What are you doing in that getup?"

Dexter stopped abruptly, turned around long enough to mumble, "no speaka the English," and hurried on his way.

"Why did you take our computer?" Morty asked. *"Can't your station afford to buy you one?"*

Dexter ran out of the building while we laughed uproariously.

We laughed again when we played back the tape, because

we had videotaped the whole thing. And we laughed again when we showed it on the six o'clock news that evening.

To Dexter, the Dean of Toledo Weathermen, this public humiliation was tantamount to a declaration of war. He apparently concluded it was time to pull out the big guns. That evening, I received a call from W.C. Muldoon.

"You have gone too far, Sheldon," he thundered. "First, you screw around with our weather. Then, you publicly humiliate Dexter Bentley, a fine human being. Dexter called and told me how you set him up. Said it's time to annihilate the enemy—namely you—once and for all. You ought to be ashamed. Such conduct is outrageous for a weatherman—"

I merely caught Dexter in the act of committing dastardly deeds. Dexter was the one who should be ashamed—he stole my weather computer, then threatened to "annihilate" me. But I didn't have a chance to tell old W.C. that because he was still rambling.

"—and you aren't going to get away with it, Sheldon. Dexter has reported you to the Committee on Ethics and Public Censure of the National Meteorological Society, and the Committee will conduct an official inquiry into your recent nefarious activities. After a fair and impartial hearing, you will be found guilty of the charges, and you will be censured. You will be publicly condemned and exposed as a fraud and a charlatan, and the Committee won't stop its campaign against you until you are officially removed from your job at WWTT."

"Would you mind running that threat by me again—the part about a 'fair and impartial hearing'?"

"This is a very serious matter, Sheldon. You might as well start looking for another line of work, because when the Committee gets done with you, *you will never again find employment as a weather forecaster!*"

Having said that, old W.C. slammed down the phone. I had the feeling he didn't plan on inviting me to the next Weatherman's Charity Ball—the biggest shindig in the Toledo meteorological fraternity, the one which usually ended about three in the morning with W.C. and Dexter singing "How Dry I Am" at the Toledo Zoo Hippoquarium as three-ton hippos mated.

Morty Greer stuck his head inside my weather cubicle.

"Hey, Jer! What kind of weather do you have lined up for this weekend?"

Holy cow. I had nearly forgotten Rev. Furrow was counting on me to arrange religiously correct weather for the church picnic Saturday.

On Friday evening's newscasts, I declared that Saturday would be mild in Toledo, with a high of 76 and a few clouds—just as the Rev. Furrow had requested.

As I was about to leave the building, Luther called.

"Are you sitting down, Jer?" he asked.

Oh, Lord, I thought. What had Luther done now?

I sat down.

"I just got a call from Hollywood. Gromighty Productions is offering a million dollars for exclusive rights to Toledo's weather and your story."

I was flabbergasted. "A million dollars?"

"That's right. If we take it, you'll be a millionaire—minus my twenty-five percent, of course."

"Fifteen percent," I corrected him.

"Whatever. What do you say?"

"Let me think about it."

"Don't think too long. We'd better take the money and run before they change their minds."

"I don't know, Luther . . ."

He had hung up.

So I would soon be a millionaire? Everything was happening so fast.

15

Between newscasts on Friday evening, I drove to The Docks, a complex that housed six restaurants, and met Laura at Cousino's Navy Bistro for dinner. Our relationship had deteriorated since she became convinced I was dabbling in something sinister and we were back at the stage where jogging in the park was more important to Laura than seeing me. I resolved to patch things up before we became more distant. I was having a great time because of my success with the weather, but without Laura, there was a void in my life. I wanted it all.

We dined outdoors overlooking the Maumee River.

"So, how was your day?" she asked, as she stabbed a fork into her Lake Superior whitefish.

"Not bad." I said, as I cut into my porterhouse steak. "I arranged the weather for Rev. Furrow's picnic, received a letter from a tribal leader in Africa begging me to send rain his way, and . . . oh, yes . . . I became a millionaire."

"A millionaire?" She was stunned.

"Well, I did, and I didn't. Luther wants to sell the film rights to my story for a million dollars, but Uncle Sam and Luther get half the money."

"Film rights? *To what? Toledo's weather? You haven't got anything to sell that belongs to you! How can you tell me you aren't trying to cash in on your gift?*"

It didn't seem like the right time to mention Luther was pursuing deals for Miracle Weatherman collector cards and a cereal box bearing my mug shot. "Don't jump to conclusions, Laura. This isn't about cashing in on a gift from God. I didn't do anything bad, or criminal." I sipped the wine and leaned back. "Do you know what this is really about? *It's my chance to make it big.* People are *giving* me the money. It's my turn to ride the bucking bronco of Success, and I'm holding on for dear life!"

"You're young, Jerry. Don't be impatient. There will be other opportunities."

"There may not be. I can't let this slip by. *This* is my chance to make my mark in the sand, to scribble my 'Kilroy was here' on the wall of history. This is my chance to be remembered for doing something incredible!"

"Why can't you forget about the money? Enjoy this special gift, as you call it, without exploiting it."

And be broke for the rest of my life? Poor Laura. Poor naive Laura. I leaned across the table and touched her hands gently as I explained the Facts of Life.

"Laura, dear, I've got to think of the future. When this is all over, what will I have? If I'm broke, I'll be back where I started. Sure, I'd have the experience of living through all this, but I'd still be a struggling weatherman at a failing Toledo television station without enough money to marry you."

"Don't use *me* as an excuse to make money out of this," Laura snapped.

"I didn't mean it that way. I believe this forecasting gift

was sent my way to help me succeed. Somebody Up There *wants me to succeed!* That means making some money while I can, so I won't be broke and struggling forever. And I want you to share my success with me, because without you, it doesn't mean anything."

I was exaggerating, of course. Without Laura, I could still enjoy the half million dollars and the fame. And yet, it would be a lot more fun if she came along for the ride. I didn't feel that way about anyone else. It must have been love—or a strong desire for a larger tax deduction.

"I don't know, Jerry. What you say makes sense, in a J. Paul Getty kind of way. I'm just not sure if it's your shot at success or you're trying to exploit a supernatural gift."

"Laura, you've got to realize all this hasn't changed me. I'm still the same Jerry Sheldon. I'm still honest and decent. Only richer."

She picked at her food a few moments, then laughed. "You never were decent. . . . All right. I suppose I owe you the chance to prove all this hasn't gone to your head. I'll let you take Kathy and me to the church picnic tomorrow, and we'll go on from there."

Notice I didn't say I wanted to go to the picnic. Nor did I invite Laura and Kathy to go with me. But Laura would let me take them. And I agreed. She had trained me well, but I could live with that. Sometimes if you want a woman to share your success, you've got to surrender part of your life as well as your billfold.

V

Storm Clouds

16

The next morning was cloudy and cooler than I expected—the temperature hovered around the 50s—but I figured Edward had slept late and would get rid of some of the clouds and crank up the heat after he had his morning coffee.

Before accompanying Laura and Kathy to the church picnic, I dropped by the WWTT building to polish up some weather graphics. I was putting final touches on an animated sequence depicting overnight lows when Reggie called to report the broadcasting convention was nearly over.

"I've learned a lot," he said. "Maybe someday, if you show enough promise and stop sending hate mail to J.P., he'll let you attend one of these things."

"Stranger things have happened," I noted. "So, you'll be back for next weekend's weather?"

"No can do," Reggie said. "J.P. wants me to stick around a while and tell him more about our operations in Toledo. I think he's grooming me for management. I'm moving up the ladder, old boy. At this rate, I'll have Pauley's job before another week passes!"

Pauley was such a basket case that I hesitated to give him that bit of news. It might push our Fearless Leader over the edge. Then I figured what the hell, he'd just need to handle it.

"My job?" Pauley bellowed, when I told him. "Why, that little traitor! I don't care if he is J.P.'s drinking buddy, he's gone too far! I'm firing him! Where should I send the telegram telling him he's fired?"

"Send it to J.P.'s office," I suggested.

Pauley sighed. That bit of information took the wind out of his sails. "All right. So I can't get rid of him. But I can make his life miserable in a hundred little ways. I didn't waste my time at Business School!"

Later that day, Laura and Kathy jumped into the old Buick and we headed to Secor Metropark for the church picnic. Secor, one of nine large metroparks scattered throughout the area, offered picnic areas, an arboretum, a trail and plenty of trees.

The heavy cloud cover had drifted eastward. Although the sun shone brightly, it hadn't warmed things up—the temperature had plunged about 10 degrees. Nevertheless, I was sure Edward would get his act together quickly and Rev. Furrow would have his ideal picnic weather.

By the time we reached the park, it was indeed a few degrees warmer. I whipped the Buick into a parking space next to Rev. Furrow's shiny new Lincoln. The preacher had just arrived with his wife, Estella.

"How do you like the car?" Rev. Furrow inquired.

"It's smashing."

"Yes, it is. I could have laid out a few more bucks for a Cadillac, but I decided against it. People might think I was getting too big for the congregation."

I had the sinking feeling my weekly church offering wasn't funding a mission in Zaire but a Lincoln in the preacher's garage. Nevertheless, I usually give clergymen the benefit of a doubt until they are convicted on twenty or thirty counts of fraud.

"It's rather cool, Jerry. Sure as Hades isn't 76. Where's that warm weather you promised me?"

"It will be here. It's warming up fast," I pointed out.

"Hmm," the preacher mumbled. "I hope so."

The Furrows grabbed picnic baskets from the back seat of the Lincoln and marched toward the picnic area. I retrieved from the back of the Buick bowls of potato salad and fruit salad that Laura had whipped up, and Laura and I followed the Furrows. Kathy trailed along at her own pace.

The temperature climbed quickly. By the time people unpacked their picnic baskets it felt like 76. But the preacher wasn't satisfied.

"All the clouds disappeared!" he hollered over to me. "I wanted a few clouds to keep it from getting too hot!"

I shrugged.

A moment later, a few stratocumulus clouds appeared on the horizon. I was surprised Edward hadn't sent me cirrus or cumulus clouds because they are generally less dense. Still, stratocumulus clouds are nothing to worry about, and I was relieved Edward had sent something our way.

I shouted to the preacher, "Clouds!" And I pointed at them.

"About time," he grumbled.

Laura unpacked paper plates, plastic forks and napkins. When she finished, she gestured toward a clump of rose bushes.

"Look at them!" she said. "Look what you've done!"

"I give up. What have I done?"

"The roses have bloomed. Robins are building nests in the trees. They think it's Spring! Your weather is screwing everything up!"

I shrugged. "Spring came early. What's the big deal? I mean, that's what the world is all about. Things change. Either you adjust or you become extinct. Look what happened to the dinosaurs."

"Yes, but they didn't have a weird weatherman screwing up their environment!"

"We really don't know that, do we, Laura? I mean, it could have happened that way. A meteorologist turned their climate upside down and *wham*—no more dinosaurs. . . . What do you think, Kathy?"

She screwed up her face as she pondered the question. "I think you should quit messing with the weather and bring back the dinosaurs."

"I'm not sure that's a good idea, honey," I said. "People today are squeamish. They go nuts when an inch-long roach shows up in their kitchen sinks, or a little mouse scampers across the living room floor. What would they do if a sixty- or eighty-foot dinosaur showed up at the door?"

Laura sighed. "I'd tell him to get rid of the roach and the mouse. . . . I was trying to make a serious point, Jerry. The weather, the seasons, the birds and the trees—they are all beyond our understanding and control. We have no business messing around with any of them. You're upsetting the delicate balance that makes life on this planet possible!"

I was responsible for *that*? Two weeks earlier, all I worried about was maintaining the delicate balance in my checking account.

While some of the church faithful spread food out on picnic tables, the rest of us took part in a ragtag game of softball. Rev. Furrow insisted on pitching. It was obvious after he walked three batters and gave up a triple and a single that pitching was not his forte, but he was more or less in charge of the affair and no one had the power to go to the mound, take the ball from him and send him to the showers—although I tried.

With four runs in and a runner on base—Wilma Jenkins, who was sitting at second base in an electric wheelchair—Kathy dug in at home plate. Rev. Furrow managed to get the pitch over the plate and Kathy smacked it, sending it dribbling to the shortstop, who bobbled it. When I stepped up to the plate, Wilma was on third and Kathy proudly occupied first.

I tugged at my cap and rubbed my hands together and did all those other things a batter is supposed to do. Then I slammed a pitch foul down the third base line, nearly knocking Wilma out of her wheelchair. She bellowed at me in colorful language that usually isn't heard at church picnics.

I stepped back from the plate, knocked dirt off my shoes with the bat and took a deep breath. Laura must have noticed my steely-eyed determination because she seemed to think I planned on nailing Wilma with the next pitch.

"Don't you dare, Jerry!" she shouted.

I heaved a heavy sigh. Laura and I definitely knew each other too well. But I was not planning on knocking Wilma out of her chair with the next pitch. I was going to send her a pop fly to see if she could catch it.

It was then I noticed the harmless stratocumulus clouds had given way to nimbostratus clouds—clouds that often produce rain—and they were moving in quickly, blocking out the sun. Evidently, Rev. Furrow noticed the same thing. He trotted in from the pitcher's mound.

"What's going on, Jerry? I requested a few light clouds. I didn't want rain! What's happening, boy? Speak to me!"

A moment later, quarter-inch hail tumbled out of the heavens.

"Good Lord, we're under attack!" he shrieked. "I thought you had control of the weather!"

"Well, I do, more or less," I insisted, as I shielded my head from the hail with my hands. "A few bugs haven't been worked out yet."

Hail pelted us as we ran over to the picnic tables and hastily gathered up the food. By the time we reached the parking lot, heavy rain was falling. The preacher quickly discovered he had neglected to roll up the windows on the Lincoln. Puddles of water lay inside the car.

"Heavens! My Lincoln looks like a swamp," he moaned, as he revved up the engine. "I'm very disappointed in you, Jerry."

"Me, too," said Kathy, who hopped, soaking wet, inside the Buick.

"So am I," chimed in Laura, whose hair looked like something out of a Godzilla movie.

"And so am I!" roared Wilma, who was being loaded into a handicap van with the help of her daughter.

I was disappointed, too. Disappointed in Edward. I thought we had a deal. I thought I had control of Toledo's weather. I would issue orders and, like a corporal in a grade B war movie, Edward would carry them out. What good was it if I had responsibility for the weather but didn't have control over it?

The rain stopped a few minutes later, but by then we were on the road back to Sylvania and the picnic had been officially and irrevocably rained out.

I was still angry about the downpour later that afternoon when I summoned Edward on my weather computer.

We had an agreement, Edward. If I'm going to be in charge of Toledo's weather, I must have full command over it.

SO WHAT'S THE PROBLEM? YOU ASKED FOR A FEW CLOUDS AND A HIGH OF 76 AND THAT'S WHAT I GAVE YOU. IT ISN'T MY FAULT THE CLOUDS SPAWNED A LITTLE RAIN AND HAIL.

That's what I'm talking about, Edward! I requested a few clouds. If I wanted hail and rain, I'd ask for them! You had weather floating in and out of Toledo like whores at a sales convention. From now on, follow my forecasts exactly. Why are you fighting me on this? Do you want me to fail?

Suddenly things seemed much clearer.

That's it, isn't it! You want me to fail! You got tired of hearing me and others complain about the job you were doing, so you wanted me to fall flat on my face. Then you would look good.

NONSENSE. WE DON'T THINK THAT WAY UP HERE.

The rest of them don't, but you do. You didn't learn tricks like that in Heaven, Edward!

WELL, NO. I LEARNED THEM IN CHICAGO.

From now on, Edward, don't play games with me. Follow my forecasts to the letter without screwing them up. Agreed?

I SUPPOSE SO. BUT JERRY, THERE REALLY IS A LOT MORE TO THIS THAN YOU KNOW. THERE ARE MANY FACTORS TO BALANCE OUT.

Just do it!

I DON'T THINK I LIKE YOU ANYMORE, JERRY.

17

I viewed the picnic disaster as a temporary setback, a minor obstacle on the road to Success. What really threw me for a loop was that I had been wrong when I told Laura that Somebody Up There wanted me to succeed. Somebody Up There was doing his best to see that I failed! The implications were staggering, so I tried not to think about them.

Once again, sleeping late was on my agenda for Sunday, but the ringing of the phone woke me at 7 A.M.

"Perhaps I was too hasty," Laura said. "I called Rev. Furrow last night. He wants you to take Kathy and me to church this morning. To show you are right with the Lord, and all."

"I'm awfully tired," I said. "Maybe I could show I'm 'right with the Lord' some other time."

"Jerry Sheldon! Don't joke about a thing like this! If there's anyone who ever needed religion, it's you!"

That seemed a little extreme—the world is populated by tens of thousands of murderers, rapists and politicians—but I knew why she said it. She thought that once I had "seen the light", I would stop messing around with God's weather.

Since I had scheduled beautiful weather for Sunday and I couldn't see any way to say no without kissing off my relationship with Laura entirely, I agreed to pick her up after I showered.

"Jerry, I told you to throw away that suit! It looks terrible! You look like an ad for 'The Beverly Hillbillies'."

I was thoroughly confused. "I did throw away the suit. This is my good one."

"No, it isn't. It's got those stupid gray checks in the design. Your good one is dark blue."

I looked at it.

"Good grief. I threw away the wrong suit! . . . It's all your fault. You nag at me about suits at sunrise on a Sunday morning and who can think that early in the morning? There's a homeless person downtown who's got my good blue suit!"

Laura shrugged. "It wasn't that great, Jerry. Buy yourself some new suits. You don't need to look like an ad for a surplus store."

We didn't talk much as I drove through sun-drenched streets to the Fourth Baptist Church.

Once inside, we made our way toward the front pews—which made me nervous because I wasn't sure if Rev. Furrow packed a gun—and settled in. Rev. Furrow sat behind the podium in a straightback chair. He looked everywhere but in my direction. Obviously, he was ignoring me.

When the preacher approached the podium to read the opening announcements, I noticed he had a sniffle. Apparently he had caught a cold when the rains came the day before. I only hoped he didn't blame me for that, too.

The services weren't far along before I sensed a theme was emerging. The opening hymn was "A Shelter in the

Time of Storm". This was followed by "There Shall Be Showers of Blessing" and "Whiter Than Snow". But perhaps I was
being paranoid, because the next hymn was "I'll Stand By
Until the Morning". I looked up the opening words in the
hymnal.

Fierce and wild the storm is raging . . .

I was right the first time. A theme definitely was emerging. I examined the listing in the church bulletin. The scrip-
ture reading came from Genesis—the verses that focus on
God, Noah and the Great Flood. After the offering, Rev.
Furrow would preach on "Tinkering With God's Plans". This
would be followed by the closing hymn, "Leaving It All to
Jesus".

It occurred to me that Rev. Furrow wouldn't have under-
taken a service built around such a strong theme unless he
was sure I would be in the pews. It definitely smacked of a
conspiracy between Laura and Rev. Furrow—a conspiracy
to show me the error of my ways and make me repent.

Rev. Furrow waited patiently while the choir leader led
the congregation in the medley of Gospel Weather Tunes.
(For a moment, I thought I might be on to something. I could
sell CDs and tapes of Gospel Weather Tunes on cable television channels. Perhaps it would bring in several thousand
dollars of extra income. Then, remembering where I was, I
apologized to God for being so materialistic in His house
and I dumped the idea. Two weeks later, ads for Gospel
Weather Tunes began running on late-night cable stations—
"just send your money to Furrow Enterprises . . ." This did
not surprise me. Rev. Furrow was a no-nonsense conserva-
tive preacher who believed in the teachings of the Bible and
the *Wall Street Journal*. His motto seemed to be, "Love Some
of Thy Neighbors and All of Thy Net Worth".)

After being uplifted by the medley of weather hymns, I threw ten dollars in the collection plate. A few moments later, the Rev. Furrow launched into his sermon.

The good preacher began by telling how God had ordered Noah to get ready for the big flood that would be coming in 120 years, and Noah heeded the Lord and built a massive ark. Rev. Furrow read from Scriptures the passage in which God says, "I will cause it to rain upon the earth forty days and forty nights, and every living substance that I have made will I destroy from off the face of the earth." When there had been enough flooding, Rev. Furrow noted, God made a wind to pass over the earth, and the waters abated.

I felt humble. This was indeed the Major Leagues of weather manipulation.

From Genesis, the preacher turned to Exodus, and the ten plagues visited upon Egypt. He focused on the seventh plague, which involved hail. God told Moses, "Behold, tomorrow about this time I will cause it to rain a very grievous hail, such as hath not been in Egypt since the foundation thereof even until now." Moses stretched forth his rod to heaven, and the Lord sent thunder and hail, and the fire ran along upon the ground, and the Lord rained hail upon the Land of Egypt.

It was about the time God rained hail on Egypt that I realized I wasn't getting the message from the sermon that the preacher intended. I was enjoying it too much. It was like a tremendously entertaining Hollywood film. I immediately buried my feelings, scolded myself and loaded myself with guilt. I'm sure that was more along the lines of the response Rev. Furrow expected.

The preacher moved along to other examples of biblical-scale weather. The point of all this was clear, but the preacher hammered it home again in case I had missed it.

"Is there any doubt that weather is the province of God and not man?" he roared. "It is sheer idiocy for mankind to think it can control the weather on God's earth—but there has been no shortage of those who have tried, for there are many lunatics roaming the planet."

Suddenly it seemed uncomfortably warm in the church, or could it be that I was perspiring excessively?

The preacher launched into a description of some of man's puny and misguided efforts to control the weather over the years. He cited a few notable examples. When a researcher at General Electric burned some silver iodide in a laboratory, the smoke drifted and started a small snowstorm in a frozen food cabinet six miles away. In 1947, planes seeded hurricane clouds over the Atlantic with seven dollars' worth of dry ice. The hurricane reversed course and pounded the city of Savannah, resulting in five million dollars in property damage.

The conclusion was clear, Rev. Furrow bellowed. Where God had excelled at weather-making, man had been a dismal failure. The spell that Toledo was under would surely end in disaster because it was not the work of God but of a "demented weatherman".

"Is Dexter Bentley here today?" I whispered to Laura.

"No! He meant *you!*"

I slumped in my seat.

After the service, Rev. Furrow hurried to the door to shake hands with parishioners as they left the church. Laura, Kathy and I were headed straight for him.

"Behave yourself," Laura whispered to me. "Don't embarrass us!"

"Well, of course not. Have a little faith in me. We're in church."

As we neared the door, I grabbed the preacher's hand and shook it. "Just wanted to let you know that the Demented Weatherman enjoyed your sermon!"

Kathy giggled as Rev. Furrow sternly responded, "I hope I gave you food for thought."

"He certainly did," I said, when Laura, Kathy and I reached the parking lot. "I was thinking it might be time to find a different church."

"You didn't hear a word Rev. Furrow said," Laura declared. "All that wisdom was wasted on a . . . a . . . a whimsical weatherman like you!"

I was amused that "whimsical weatherman" was the worst thing Laura could say about me, but she was new to the defamation game. She could never make it on the streets of a big city. When she saw that I wasn't taking her seriously she didn't say another word as I drove her and Kathy home. I had the feeling the wedding had been postponed another year or two.

18

Rev. Furrow and Laura were not the only ones giving me grief.

The Aerovane indicator at my house recorded winds of 126 miles an hour the following morning. A light breeze rippled through the trees outside, but I think I would have noticed if the winds were that strong. There was only one explanation. Hard Head McCullough had struck again. I put on slippers and a bathrobe and paddled out to my back-porch.

"Hard Head! … Hey! Old Man McCullough!"

"Whatdyawant, Weatherman?"

"What did you do to my Aerovane transmitter?"

"Your what?"

"My wind measurement gizmo." I pointed to the transmitter. *"The thing that looks like an airplane."*

"I don't play with toys, Weatherman. I leave that up to you."

I noticed the propeller that measured wind speed had been torn completely off the transmitter. When I looked back at Hard Head, he was blow drying his head. What's wrong with this picture? I thought. Hard Head has very little hair.

Why is he blow drying his hair? Then I realized what had happened. He had crept into my yard and held a souped-up hair dryer up to the Aerovane propeller. He had blown my little propeller to bits.

"That does it!" I said. *"I tried to live in peace with you and it doesn't work. It's time to take the gloves off. You're going down!"*

He chuckled. *"Yeah? And what are ya going to do, Weatherman?"*

I smiled. *"Did you ever hear of Mrs. Bodecker?"*

He looked puzzled as I stomped back inside my house.

That afternoon, Ruth Lanson of the National Meteorological Society called from Washington.

"Dexter Bentley and W.C. Muldoon have some rather alarming things to say about you and the weather in Toledo, Mr. Sheldon. They have asked us to take immediate action."

"I wouldn't put too much stock in what Dexter says. You're talking about a man who took seven years to graduate from the Toledo Weather College—and they only have a two-year course. And W.C. has been working at the Weather Service so long he can't remember how to get home at night. He lives at the Weather Service building."

"Nevertheless, serious charges have been leveled against you. And *something* must be altering Toledo's weather. We were willing to believe it was a fluke at first, Mr. Sheldon, but the situation appears to be much more serious than that. We will be sending a team to Toledo on Thursday afternoon to hold a public hearing, and if we find anything irregular, we will be forced to take immediate action."

"What action? I've already been banned from the Meteorological Society for life. Are you going to take away my weather maps? Decree that I can give the high temperatures but not the lows? You don't have the power to do that!"

"You'd be surprised what we can do, Mr. Sheldon. Don't forget the power of publicity. It made you and it can break you. We can publicly censure and humiliate you!"

"For giving an accurate forecast?"

"It worked with Irving Krick. In your case, we might go further. When we're finished, you won't be able to get a fore-casting job anywhere in the country!"

"Big deal. When I tried to find a new job last year, I couldn't find any. You'll have to do better than that."

"Mr. Sheldon, I don't really care for your attitude. If the hearing turns up anything illegal, or anything smacking of devil worship or witchcraft, you will be in very serious trouble! Your credibility will be zero. You won't be able to land a job wiping the johns at McDonald's."

"I wouldn't want to take Dexter's part-time work away from him. Look, Miss Lanson, there's nothing irregular about my forecasting. All this splendid Toledo weather was simply a fluke. Perhaps instead of investigating me, your Society should investigate how to duplicate Toledo's fine weather so the entire country could enjoy it."

"You can have your say at the hearing on Thursday, Mr. Sheldon. I suggest you bring an attorney with you."

I could tell Miss Lanson meant business. I reached for a telephone book, opened the yellow pages to the attorney listings and picked out a name at random—Harry Delaney. I called his office and made an appointment to see him the next day.

Despite setbacks such as the church picnic disaster, the impending public hearing and Edward's efforts to undermine my weather forecasts, I attempted to focus on positive developments.

Luther called me at work late Monday afternoon.

"We're ready to sign the papers," he announced.

"What papers?"

"Selling the film rights. The production company is putting the package together now. A screenwriter at a detox center in New Jersey is doing the script. What do you think—should we call it *Nothing But Fair Skies,* after the old song?"

"Sure, why not," I said. "But what's this about a screenwriter at a detox center? How can he write about me if he's never met me? How can he give a truthful version of everything that's happened?"

The word "truthful" alarmed Luther.

"That's the last thing we want!" he insisted. "No offense, kid, but you're not exactly Evel Knievel or Charlie Manson. We've got to make you interesting. We're after a good story. It doesn't matter if it's like real life. Most of the time real life is dull, complicated and inconclusive. Don't butt into things that are none of your business. Let me handle the details. You stick to the weather."

"But Luther, it's my life. I really think—"

"Look, Jer, we don't have to make a decision on this right now. Think it over. Besides, I've got other irons in the fire. I'm talking to the Toledo City Council about signing you to an exclusive contract. For a million a year or so, you give them the weather they want."

"A weather contract with the city? No, Luther, that's out of the—"

"You're right. Two million."

"You're missing the point, Luther. It's not right to sign . . . *two million a year? You think so?"*

"Absolutely, baby!"

I recalled what happened to Charles Warren Hatfield, a famous rainmaker who signed a contract with drought-stricken San Diego in 1916. After Hatfield spewed chemicals into the air, twenty inches of rain fell nearby, destroying a dam and causing seventeen deaths and millions of dollars in damage. The city gave Hatfield the choice of assuming liability for the deaths and damages, or fleeing without his money. He fled.

"I don't know, Luther."

"Oh-oh. Gotta hang up. Shaq O'Neal is on the other line."

"We need to talk about this, Luther!"

"Right. We'll do lunch. My secretary will set it up with your secretary."

I suppose we never "did lunch" because I didn't have a secretary.

Hard Head McCullough's mutilation of my wind-measuring instrument remained fresh in my mind that evening when I aired the forecast . . .

"OUR UNSEASONABLY MILD AND ENJOYABLE WEATHER WILL CONTINUE TOMORROW, WITH SUNNY SKIES, JUST A FEW CLOUDS AND A HIGH OF 79—EXCEPT AT H.H. MCCULLOUGH'S RESIDENCE ON ATWELL ROAD, WHERE A BLIZZARD WILL DUMP TWO FEET OF SNOW. WE INDEED LIVE IN STRANGE TIMES."

Brent nodded. "AND THEY GET STRANGER EVERY TIME YOU GIVE THE WEATHER. NOW, TURNING TO SPORTS, MORTY GREER WILL TELL US HOW THE DETROIT PISTONS FARED AGAINST THE BULLS IN CHICAGO TONIGHT . . ."

19

Hummingbirds in nearby trees warbled cheerfully as an alarm clock interrupted my slumber the next morning. I liked this alarm clock better than my old one. Instead of a blaring alarm or raucous radio music, it played an audio tape I had recorded . . .

"Jerry, if you want to get up, it's eight-thirty. It's a gorgeous day and you are a terrific weatherman—one of the greatest meteorologists of all time. You are also handsome, intelligent and incredibly sexy."

For some unexplainable reason, the tape put me in a better mood.

As I headed for the shower, I glanced out the window into the backyard. The sun was shining in my yard, but over in Hard Head's yard a vicious blizzard piled up mounds of snow. The old bag of bones, bundled in a shabby overcoat and a hunter's cap with ear flaps, was shoveling snow off his sidewalk.

I opened the window.

"Beautiful day, isn't it, Hard Head!"

He shook a fist at me. *"Beulah Morgan was right. You are a low-down, despicable roach! Come on over here and I'll bury you under a ton of this stuff."*

"That'll teach you to mess around with the maestro," I said.

One thing was sure—I couldn't count on Hard Head to be a character witness for me when the Meteorological Society convened its witchhunt.

At WWTT, Pauley and Brent accosted me as I entered the newsroom.

Pauley growled, "What did you do now?"

So much had happened over the previous two weeks I didn't know what he was referring to.

"Could you be more specific?" I said.

Brent shoved that morning's *Blade* in front of me. On the front page below the fold appeared a story with a three-column headline:

Meteorological Society Hearing To Determine Sheldon's Fate

"It says a Committee on Ethics and Public Censure is convening here Thursday afternoon to consider blackballing you from any type of meteorological work," Brent said. "What happened—did you shoot Dexter Bentley?"

"It's nothing. This is something Dexter and W.C. Muldoon cooked up. I haven't done anything wrong!"

Brent shook his head. "That's what Nixon said, right up to the end. I'll give you the same advice I gave Dick: get out of town while you still can."

"J.P. isn't going to like this," Pauley whined. "If you and your miracle weather forecasts go belly up, he'll sell us or shut us down for sure. This could be the last straw."

"Don't panic yet, Pauley. I'm still handling the weather and I've got a lawyer. We'll get through this."

"That's what Nixon said," Brent noted.

I was halfway to the weather room when Pauley yelled, "By the way, Sheldon. Who's paying for the lawyer? I don't want to see any expense sheets for 'one attorney—ten thousand dollars'."

I had planned to slip the expense voucher to Pauley after the hearing, but it looked like I would need to come up with another approach.

I wanted Laura to hear about the hearing from me, not from newspaper headlines. I knew she had the day off so I called her house. Laura said she planned to spend the day Christmas shopping at the Franklin Park Mall. I agreed to meet her at the Lion Department Store and buy her lunch at the mall.

As I drove to the northwest suburbs of Toledo, the radio reported the temperature was 71, "headed for a high—according to Jerry Sheldon—of precisely 79 degrees". As I parked in the mall lot, I noticed several shoppers clad in shorts heading for the entrances.

The mall, which housed more than a hundred stores and shops, was not crowded. I didn't need to ask store managers how Christmas retail sales were going. I could read their faces as though they were barometers. They were glum. Sales had dipped considerably.

In the Lion Department Store, I found Laura rummaging through a table of sweaters. She picked out a pink one for Kathy. Then, we browsed through the toy department, where my eyes were drawn to a new item—a Toledo Weatherman Doll.

I was holding it in my hands, confronting it face to face, when Laura came up behind me.

"Really, Jerry. Is there no end? Toledo Weatherman Dolls? What's next? Toledo Weatherman Underwear?"

"Remind me not to let you go near the underwear section."

She looked at the doll I was holding more closely. "It looks just like you."

The doll was a foot and a half high, with curly brown hair and a stupid grin. In his pockets were a little thermometer and barometer. I thought the doll looked like a hick, but it was money in the bank, so who was I to complain?

"They're selling like hotcakes," a saleslady said, as she came over and straightened up the stack of boxes holding the dolls. "Don't ask me why."

"They're obviously the perfect gift," I suggested. "They're cute, they have a local significance, they're something a kid can hang onto forever."

The clerk took another look at the doll. Apparently it didn't look any better to her. "Are you drunk?" she asked me.

She picked up a Patsy Pearl doll from a nearby shelf. "Now, this is a much better value for the money. Same price, but this one sheds real tears and pees."

I scrutinized the box containing the Toledo Weatherman Doll. "It says here he washes his own face and poops," I lied.

The clerk looked shocked. *"What?"*

Laura hurried me toward the exit. "Please excuse him. Sometimes he forgets his manners."

The clerk took a good look at me. "You know, he looks a little like the doll. Same stupid grin."

In the mall's food court, we ordered hot dogs and sat at a small table with a view of the mall.

"Admit it, Jerry," Laura said. "It's ridiculous to be Christmas shopping during a heat wave. We should be trudging through snow with bundles of beautifully wrapped packages, then hurrying home to warm up by drinking hot chocolate. I can't get in the mood for Christmas shopping when air conditioners are running!"

I understood what she was saying. Christmas carols piped through a mall don't have the same effect on the soul when you're wearing shorts and sporting a tan. And many Toledo children—including Kathy—were giving me the cold shoulder. They figured it was time for sledding, snowball fights and ice skating. Every time I saw her, Kathy asked if we would have a white Christmas. I wanted to say yes, but I couldn't promise. I didn't know if I would still be running the weather at Christmas.

"If you really are in charge of the weather," Laura said, as a couple in matching turquoise sweatsuits hurried by, "why don't you do something about it? Why don't you cool it off?"

I shrugged. How could I explain that I was afraid to forecast snow and cold weather because Edward might go overboard? Every time I varied the forecast, disaster struck. Breezes turned into damage-causing winds. Fog led to serious automobile accidents. A few clouds led to hail and heavy rain. If I called for snow, Toledo could be buried under thirty or forty inches of the white stuff.

"I think it's better if I don't mess with the weather too much until I get some of the kinks worked out," I said. I changed the subject. "By the way, there's a minor, insignificant little thing I probably should mention before you read about it in the newspapers."

"Oh? And what is that?" she asked warily.

"Nothing much really. A committee is coming to town Thursday to hold a public hearing. They want to stop me from ever working in the weather business again."

"*What?*"

"Yeah. No big deal. Dexter and W.C. want them to hang me out to dry. Pass the ketchup, would you?"

"Well, what are you going to do about it?"

"The main attraction at a lynching doesn't need to do much. He shows up, and they lynch him."

Laura munched on her hot dog as a Santa Claus in red shorts roller-bladed by.

"Well, you'll defend yourself, won't you? You'll tell them how wrong they are?"

"Aren't you the lady who accused me of dabbling in something sinful or demonic?"

"Yes, but I'm your fianceé. I can do that. Besides, I think you got mixed up in all this out of ignorance. They probably think you did it intentionally and maliciously. What are you going to tell the committee?"

"Would they believe me if I said I had a pipeline to Heaven?"

"They'd murder you."

I sighed. "Yeah. That's what I thought."

"If I were you, I'd quit screwing with the weather."

"Absolutely. Toledo will be cool from now until the committee arrives, but no thunderstorms, blizzards, or anything like that. Nothing to rock the boat. Nothing that could cause damage or stir up passions against me."

As Laura walked me to my car, she stopped and kissed me. "Kathy and I will be at the hearing to support you," she said.

"Have I taken the time since all this began to tell you that I love you?"

Laura smiled. "Why did I fall for a man who thinks he's got a pipeline to Heaven?"

"Because that's what you like about me. You wouldn't be happy with someone who wanted to work all his life at a struggling little TV station just reading the forecast."

I detected a mischievous twinkle in her eyes. "Don't be so sure. Dexter Bentley is looking better to me every day."

"You are one sick chick. Forget my problems. Let's get serious help for you."

Laura laughed. "Oh, by the way, Jerry, I made an appointment to have my hair done at three. Would you mind picking Kathy up after school and watching her? She could go to the station with you. She loves that!"

So many things were going wrong in my life that I had no desire to be saddled with babysitting a nine year old. But since I wanted to strengthen my relationship with Laura, and Kathy was never any trouble, I agreed to do it.

"What type of hair work are we talking here? Minor repairs or a major overhaul? Will it take hours, days or months?"

"You're on very thin ice," Laura said.

"Kathy and I will have a fine time," I assured her. "Don't worry about it. If she gets bored, she can go into Pauley's office and run the station."

As I drove from the mall to Harry Delaney's law office on the north side of the city, I discovered Toledo's discontent with my weather forecasting had bubbled over into Ralph and Malinda's drive-time radio show. One caller in particular got my attention …

"I'VE HAD ABOUT ALL I CAN TAKE OF THAT ARROGANT AIRHEAD WEATHERMAN. IF I WANTED WEATHER LIKE THIS, I'D MOVE TO THE TROPICS. GIVE ME BACK MY SNOW, SLUSH, ICE AND BONE-CHILLING TEMPERATURES. SEND THE WEATHERMAN TO LOS ANGELES OR HAWAII!"

I nearly swerved into a utility pole. The caller had a terrific idea! In the next few minutes, though, nobody followed up on it. I didn't think such a meritorious proposal should be ignored. I pulled into a convenience store parking lot and rushed to a pay phone, where I called Malinda and Ralph.

After three or four minutes, I was on the air. I disguised my voice . . .

"SAY, FOLKS . . . THE CALLER WHO SUGGESTED WE SEND THAT ARROGANT AIRHEAD WEATHERMAN TO HAWAII HAD THE RIGHT IDEA. I'D LIKE TO BE THE FIRST TO CONTRIBUTE TO THE FUND. I'LL SEND IN A HUNDRED DOLLARS!"

"WE'LL MAKE A NOTE OF THAT," Ralph said. "IF NO ONE ELSE PLEDGES MONEY, MAYBE WE COULD GET JERRY SHELDON A BUS TICKET TO PEORIA! ANYTHING TO GET HIM OUT OF TOWN. RIGHT?"

Good grief. Just what I needed—to spend a hundred bucks of my money on a bus ticket to central Illinois. I was a bit ashamed of myself for scheming to get a paid vacation to Hawaii, but I continued to listen to Malinda and Ralph as I drove. No one else contributed to my vacation fund. A number of people suggested I get out of town, but they were unwilling to put up the money.

20

As my Buick headed down Stickney Avenue toward Harry Delaney's law offices, I recalled the story about how the avenue had gotten its name. It was named for two brothers, One Stickney and Two Stickney. When Michigan and Ohio faced off in "the Toledo War" of 1835-36 over a strip of land both of them claimed, the only casualty had been a Michigan deputy sheriff stabbed by Two Stickney when One Stickney was arrested. I wondered if somewhere in Michigan there was an avenue named for the deputy sheriff who had died. (Incidentally, Ohio got the land; Michigan was given the Upper Peninsula.)

Harry Delaney's law practice shared space with a barber shop and a delicatessen in a deteriorating brick building on Stickney Avenue. I climbed a flight of creaking stairs to reach his bailiwick.

From the moment I opened the door, it was obvious I was not in the domain of a high-priced corporate lawyer. The maroon rug was shabby from wear, the furniture scratched and chipped. There was no waiting room or reception area.

"May I help you?" a young brunette asked, as she set aside a tattered copy of *People* magazine. Apparently she was Delaney's secretary.

"I'm Jerry Sheldon."

A bearded, lanky middle-aged man working at a scarred oak desk at the other end of the room scrutinized me. He rose to his feet and approached me.

"When I saw your name on my appointment sheet, I didn't realize you were The Weatherman . . ."

The Weatherman. Yes, people were beginning to know me.

". . . I wouldn't have agreed to see you," he mumbled.

"Why not?" I asked.

He gestured toward a chair a few feet in front of his desk. I sat down.

"I heard about the public hearing scheduled for Thursday. I presume that's why you are here."

"That's right."

"I was thinking about showing up at the hearing—for the other side."

I had never seen Delaney before. What had I done to alienate him?

He gazed out the window as fluffy clouds fluttered by. "Remember the hailstorm that passed through town Saturday?"

The day of the Church Picnic Disaster. How could I forget?

"The hail left little craters all over my car. It will cost me four hundred bucks to get it repaired. I told my insurance agent, 'I've got disaster insurance. It's supposed to insure me against acts of God.' He said I was right—but the policy doesn't cover acts by a Crazy Weatherman."

"Look, I'm sorry about that, Harry, but you're talking about something that was out of my control. You've been reading too many hyped-up stories about me. I'm just a meteorologist who happens to be more accurate than the other weathermen in town."

He studied my face for signs that I was lying. "A lot of people are convinced you created this weather."

"And you believe them? Maybe you're too gullible to be a lawyer."

He thought that over.

I persisted. "I need an attorney at the hearing to defend me and protect me against ridiculous, unfounded accusations."

He sighed. I thought he might be thinking about the legal aspects of my plight, but I was wrong.

"Heard about your movie deal—" he said.

"Yes . . ."

"—and the money you're going to get."

"I won't get a million. By the time the government and my agent take their shares, I'll be lucky to get half."

"Uh-huh. Well, I guess you can afford me."

"I don't know if you should be my attorney. You don't like me and you don't believe I'm innocent."

"That's not important. If I only defend clients I like or believe to be innocent, I'd starve to death."

He didn't seem to be doing all that great as it was.

"So how much would you charge to represent me?" I inquired meekly.

"Four hundred dollars an hour for the research I've got to do and the same for the hearing."

"That's not too bad. I won't need you after the hearing on Thursday."

"Right. Well, let's get started. I may have to put in a couple of all-nighters workin' on your case. . . . Incidentally, do you know how I arrived at the fee of four hundred dollars?"

"No."

"Because that's what it's going to cost me to get my car fixed!"

"Are you related to Luther Chambers, by any chance?"

"Never heard of him. So tell me, Sheldon . . . how did you manage to screw up Toledo's weather?"

21

When I pulled into the elementary school parking lot in mid-afternoon, Kathy was waiting. She threw her books into the back of the Buick and chomped on a Snickers bar.

"Your mother's getting her hair done," I explained. "You can go to the office with me."

"All right, Jerry. Is this one of those deals where she spends all evening in the beauty shop?"

"Yep. A major overhaul."

Kathy had visited the station with me on several occasions and she knew her way around.

"Well, Kathy!" Brent Lassiter exclaimed. "We haven't seen you for months. Are you the new weekend weather girl?"

Kathy grimaced. "No. I want *your* job."

"You'll have to fight me for it. And I'm bigger than you are!" Brent said jovially.

"Yes, but I'm smarter," Kathy mumbled, as I dragged her into my weather cubicle. Kathy got her moxie from her mother.

"You shouldn't be rude to Brent," I said.

"But I *am* smarter than him."

"So is everyone else in town, but you shouldn't go around telling him that."

Kathy ransacked the drawers in my desk, then settled into the chair in front of the computer as I listened to messages on my voice mail.

Two or three minutes later, she asked, "How do you spell 'snowstorm'?"

I spelled it.

"Is twenty-eight degrees a good high for the day when you have a snowstorm?"

"Uh-huh," I said. "Look, honey, don't bother me now. I'm trying to get these messages off the voice mail. I'll be finished in a minute."

A few seconds later, I realized what Kathy had asked me. "Uh, what are you doing, Kathy?"

I walked over and examined the computer monitor .

```
GIVE ME TOMORROW'S FORECAST, HOT SHOT.
Don't call me Hot Shot.
LOOK, I DON'T HAVE ALL DAY. JUST GIVE ME TOMOR-
ROW'S FORECAST.
Let's have a snowstorm, and it will be colder.
High of 28.
HOW MUCH SNOW?
A lot.
HAVE YOU BEEN DRINKING, JERRY? QUIT FOOLING
AROUND AND GIVE ME A NUMBER.
Seven inches.
O.K. SIGNING OFF.
```

"Oh, no!" I said. "You gave Edward the forecast?"

"Who is Edward?" asked Kathy.

"The one who asked for the forecast. You said it would snow!"

"Yes." She laughed.

"But—you can't do that! *I* do the forecasting around here! . . . Why did you say it would snow?"

"I'm tired of all this hot weather," Kathy explained.

I sat down and cleared the computer screen. Frantically, I tried to get Edward's attention.

```
Cancel that forecast, Edward. It was a mistake.
Cancel the forecast!!!
```

No response. I typed in a new forecast. Nothing happened. The computer had accepted Kathy's forecast and it would not accept another one. No matter what I did, I couldn't get any response.

I hoped Toledo could take it. Tuesday had been sunny, with a high of 82. In the next twenty-four hours, a raging snowstorm would dump seven inches of snow on the city. And not only were the citizens of Toledo in for a rough ride—I was, too. The lynching committee from the Meteorological Society would arrive the day after Kathy's snowstorm. If they looked on the drastic change in the weather as proof I was screwing up the climate, Kathy's snowstorm might get me booted out of the weather business.

When I took Kathy home to Sylvania that evening, Laura asked if Kathy had enjoyed playing in my office.

"It was swell," she said.

"You might want to get out your winter coat and have it ready," I suggested.

"Why?" Laura asked.

"Well, your daughter decided to forecast tomorrow's weather. Seven inches of snow will fall on Toledo."

"What? How could you let that happen?"

I shrugged. "I had nothing to do with it. She punched the thing out on the computer before I could stop her."

"Jerry Sheldon, how dare you involve Kathy in whatever weird things you're into! She's just a little girl!"

"I didn't involve her in anything. She typed in a forecast on the computer. That was all there was to it. Nothing weird about it at all."

"That's right," Kathy said. "Edward said, 'Give me tomorrow's weather forecast, Hot Shot' and I gave it to him."

"Edward? You mentioned him before, Jerry. Who's Edward? What does he have to do with this?"

"He's in the computer," Kathy said.

Laura glared at me. "You're not into anything weird, huh? What is Edward doing in the computer?"

"He's not in the computer. He's on the other end. He's the one who takes the forecast, checks to see if he has the weather in inventory, then ships it to us the next day."

"And that's not weird?"

"I was joking. He doesn't ship it to us. I come up with the forecast and Edward makes it come true. That's all there is to it. Honest."

Laura counted to ten and attempted to regain her composure. Finally, she said, "All right. I'll give you the benefit of a doubt. If you say you aren't into anything weird, I believe you. . . . Do you really think Kathy's forecast will come true?"

"Absolutely. A lot of people have been asking for a change in the weather. We'll see how they handle it tomorrow."

22

My recollections of The Day The Snow Fell are clouded by frustration and confusion.

Four inches of snow had tumbled out of the heavens by the time I pulled myself out of bed, and it was still snowing. My plan for bestowing cool but uneventful weather on Toledo before the Meteorological Society hearing was dead.

A glance out my living room window revealed something had crashed into my Buick. Judging by the size of the crater, it must have been a Mack truck.

I threw a leather coat over my pajamas and ventured outside in my slippers to inspect the damage. My little Buick had been wounded by a hit-and-run driver with an evil heart. I breathed easier when I noticed a note on the windshield. The driver apparently had left his or her name and the name of their insurance company. I grabbed the note and read it.

Serves you right, Weatherman!

That sent my blood pressure up a few dozen points.

I figured the culprit had to be a neighbor who knew the

Buick was mine. I tore the note into small pieces and hollered at the top of my voice . . .

"Listen up, you turkeys! I want the low-down, despicable, blood-sucking creature who did this to my car to come out and face me! C'mon, you craven coward! Judgment Day is here!"

A half dozen neighbors peeked out their curtains to see who the maniac was who was yelling. No one came out to face me.

A few moments later, I noticed a snowplow barrelling down the street in my direction. The driver hollered:

"Hey, buddy! Ya ain't supposed to park on the street! Don't you know there's a snow emergency?"

Then he buried my Buick under a mound of the white stuff.

"Thanks for pointing that out, idiot," I grumbled.

The numbing cold had begun to penetrate my consciousness when Beulah Morgan barged out of her house and began shoveling her walk across the street. She was bundled in a parka. Snow was still piling up, and since we were going to get three more inches, I wasn't sure why she bothered to shovel. She noticed me watching her.

"Weatherman! I want to talk to you!"

She marched toward me carrying the shovel like a pitchfork. I retreated to the safety of my front porch.

"I don't like snow, Weatherman," Beulah screamed, *"and before you forecast it again, you'd better clear it with me!"*

Safely inside my abode, I opened a window and hollered: *"I'll send a snowstorm your way whenever I feel like it. You'd better get inside! I feel a bad one coming on!"*

She scrambled back to her side of the street bellyaching, *"You're a witch, Jerry Sheldon, and I'm going to report you to the police!"*

I was ashamed of my unprofessional conduct, but I was in no mood to be messed with.

When I returned to my house, the phone rang.

"Jerry, baby. What's going on?"

It was Luther Chambers.

"Do you really think ordering up a blizzard was a smart thing to do, Jer? We were on the verge of closing a deal for a television series. We were so close I could almost touch the three hundred grand."

"Three hundred grand? You told me they wouldn't give us more than two hundred grand."

"Let's not quibble over details, Jer. You may have blown it! We may not get a dime! If you alienate people, no one will touch the project!"

"Well, Luther, baby, it isn't a blizzard. It's a snowstorm. Blizzards are accompanied by high winds."

"Blizzard, smizzard, it's all the same to Hollywood, Jer. Don't serve up any more nasty weather or you'll be left out in the cold, so to speak. If you get the urge to do this again, clear it with me first!"

Why did everyone seem to think I had to check with them before I ordered up a snowstorm?

Shortly after noon, I climbed into my Skylark. It still drove, so I decided not to leave it at the garage because the mechanic said he couldn't fix the dent for three or four months. I was tempted, though, because that was faster service than he usually provided.

The roads were a mess. Five inches of snow had blanketed Toledo, which meant we still had another two inches to go before Edward shut off the spigots. Streets were slushy and icy. Cars slid in all directions. At Detroit Avenue, a

Datsun nearly sideswiped me. Fortunately, it plowed into a discount store instead. At Jefferson Avenue, I couldn't stop and zoomed through the intersection as the light turned red. I narrowly averted a head-on with a snow removal truck. I suppose Toledoans would have considered it poetic justice if that was the way I died.

I switched on the radio to find out whether Malinda and Ralph had received any more contributions to the Fly Jerry Sheldon to Hawaii Fund. Ralph was delivering the news. Kathy's snowstorm was the top story:

"BY NOW YOU KNOW TOLEDO'S WEATHER CHANGED ABRUPTLY OVERNIGHT. AFTER TWO WEEKS OF DELIGHTFUL DAYS WITH HIGHS IN THE 70S AND 80S, A SNOWSTORM HAS DUMPED FIVE INCHES OF SNOW ON THE CITY—AND MORE IS EXPECTED. MANY TOLEDOANS WERE CAUGHT OFF-GUARD BY THE STORM. THEY HADN'T HEARD JERRY SHELDON'S FORECAST CALLING FOR SEVEN INCHES OF SNOW TODAY. SCORES OF FENDER-BENDERS HAVE BEEN REPORTED. SCHOOLS ARE CLOSED. THE ODD THING IS THAT TWENTY MILES IN ANY DIRECTION, SKIES ARE CLEAR, THOUGH TEMPERATURES ARE SEASONABLY COOL, IN THE UPPER 30S. IF YOU HAVE ANY COMPLAINTS ABOUT THE SNOW, WRITE TO JERRY SHELDON, NOT THIS STATION."

My popularity had plummeted. There was one small consolation. The forecast I delivered on the air the evening before—Kathy's forecast—had been right on the money.

When I arrived in the WWTT newsroom, a chill could be felt *inside* the building, too.

Morty, who had planned a round of golf that afternoon, was blunt. "Did you sell out, Jerry? Are you getting a kickback from snow removal and auto repair companies?"

The turn of events also annoyed Brent Lassiter. He had planned a picnic with his girlfriend—not his wife—by the lake.

"Thanks a lot, Jer," he grumbled. "A picnic didn't seem like a good idea because several inches of snow covered our favorite spot. You really screwed up this time, pal. If you can't handle the weather, you'd better let someone else do it. Dexter Bentley, maybe. I've always admired him."

"That doesn't surprise me," I said. "Actually, pal, I didn't screw up. The weather is exactly what I forecast it would be, as you would know if you had listened to my weather segment last night instead of covering your double chin with more makeup."

As I hurried to my weather room, Brent roared, *"Get Pauley Sherman. I want to see him now!"*

My voice mail and e-mail messages should have been rated "X" that afternoon. Numerous drivers who had been involved in accidents threatened to beat me up. Other Toledoans complained that their plans for outdoor activities had been spoiled. Merchants, who had been clamoring for colder temperatures to lure Christmas shoppers, were irate because the snow had screwed up traffic so badly nobody could get to the stores.

Judging by the tone of the messages and the vivid language, I could forget about running for president. I was no longer the popular, magical weatherman. I was The Enemy. John Whitaker Watson, author of the poem "Beautiful Snow", had been hung in effigy after the Blizzard of 1888. I feared the same fate awaited me.

Weather maps confirmed that everyone in the region outside Toledo was enjoying a break in the storm pattern. It was 42 in Detroit and 44 in Cleveland, with sunny skies. But a low pressure cell had settled smack on top of Toledo and smothered us in snow.

Dexter Bentley called a few minutes later. "Now what did you do to the weather?"

I chuckled. "Dexter, do you know how ridiculous you're being? I don't have an airplane. I can't seed clouds to produce snow. I don't have any voodoo powers. I didn't do anything to the weather—although my forecast was much more accurate than yours."

"I don't like you, Sheldon. You're very strange. But you'll pay for what you've done tomorrow when the Meteorological Society hit team comes to town."

"I know. Ruth Lanson called the other day. I assured her everything was fine over here, but I would help her gather the evidence she needs to have you locked up in a quiet institution where there are no television sets, and the patients cut bread with spoons because they aren't allowed to handle knives."

"Spoons, eh? How come you know so much about places like that, Sheldon?"

"I checked it out. I wouldn't have you committed to an institution without first investigating the facilities. By the way, they've got a patient ping pong tournament every Tuesday afternoon. You'll love it."

"Have fun now. After tomorrow, you'll be looking for a new job. Maybe a greasy spoon that serves chili will hire you."

I tried to explain to Edward the reason for the abrupt change in the weather so he wouldn't think I had gone psycho on him.

```
I didn't call for the snowstorm. Someone else did.
I tried to tell you it was a mistake, but you
didn't answer my message.
```

YOU THINK I'VE GOT NOTHING TO DO BUT SIT AROUND HEAVEN WAITING FOR YOUR MESSAGES? I'VE GOT ALL SORTS OF IMPORTANT THINGS TO DO. YOU HAVE CONTROL OF TOLEDO'S WEATHER. I HANDLE THE WEATHER EVERYWHERE ELSE--EXCEPT THE SEATTLE AREA. DID I TELL YOU ABOUT THAT?

Yes, you did.

TERRIFIC. I'M NOT ONLY OVERWORKED, I'M ALSO FLIRTING WITH SENILITY.

Edward, would you please check for messages more often? It might be something important.

I'LL TRY. YOU NAG ME MORE THAN MY SECOND WIFE. . . . BY THE WAY, I ASKED YOU NOT TO TELL ANYONE ABOUT ME. YOU TOLD LAURA AND KATHY.

How did you find out?

UP HERE, THEY KNOW EVERYTHING. NOT ME PERSONALLY. I HAVE TROUBLE REMEMBERING MY NAME SOMETIMES. BUT OTHERS, LIKE GOD . . . THEY KNOW EVERYTHING.

Are you angry with me for telling Laura?

DOES SHE HAVE HER OWN TALK SHOW?

No.

I SUPPOSE I CAN LET IT GO. BUT DON'T TELL ANYONE ELSE!

It was time to give Edward the forecast for Thursday. Because the Meteorological Society's headhunters would be in town, I would play it safe. With my career at stake, I didn't need any complications.

Here's the forecast, Edward. Are you ready?

LET'S HAVE IT.

For Thursday: Warmer. A few clouds. High 47. Nothing complicated. Just a nice, mild day to melt the snow.

OK. IT'S YOUR FUNERAL.

What? What do you mean, Edward? Tell me what you
mean!

I didn't receive a reply. The Weatherman in the Sky was no
longer online. Why did he say "it's your funeral"? I forecast
a cool day with a few clouds. Certainly my forecast was
harmless enough.

The snowstorm topped the "News at 6" Wednesday evening. Brent emphasized the savage effects of the storm:

"IT WAS A ROUGH DAY FOR TOLEDOANS AS A MAJOR SNOWSTORM
CLOBBERED THE CITY, SNARLING TRAFFIC AND CAUSING DOZENS OF
ACCIDENTS. I-475 WAS CLOSED FOR AN HOUR. JUST A FEW MILES AWAY,
IN WATERVILLE, RESIDENTS ENJOYED CLEAR SKIES AND TEMPERATURES
IN THE 40S. JERRY SHELDON WAS THE ONLY FORECASTER TO PREDICT
THIS DRAMATIC TURNAROUND IN OUR WEATHER. IRONICALLY, THAT
MAY BE WHAT GETS HIM INTO TROUBLE. MANY DRIVERS WHO WERE
INVOLVED IN ACCIDENTS HAVE CALLED THREATENING TO SUE YOU AND
THE STATION, JERRY."

Brent had waited until we were on the air to give me that
information.

"I DON'T BELIEVE A TELEVISION STATION HAS EVER BEEN HELD
RESPONSIBLE FOR THE WEATHER," I said. "IT'S USUALLY CONSIDERED
AN ACT OF GOD."

"BUT EVERYONE SAYS THAT YOU DO MORE THAN FORECAST THE
WEATHER—THAT YOU ACTUALLY CREATE IT."

"PROVE IT!" I snapped.

Pauley Sherman was going nuts down in the Control
Booth. I could hear him through my earphone.

"Happy Talk! What's the matter with you guys? Are you
crazy? Give me Happy Talk!"

As I drove over snow-packed roads that evening, I tried to
come up with a plan that would save my job. I thought of

one, but couldn't carry it out because it involved murdering Dexter Bentley and W.C. Muldoon. I still had a few scruples left.

I didn't go home because I didn't want to be alone. I headed for Laura's house in Sylvania. She knew what I was going through, and she was more sympathetic now. She had to be, because it was her kid who unloaded seven inches of snow on Toledo. But I didn't bring that up.

Laura consoled me and we made love until Kathy opened the bedroom door to see what all the racket was.

Later, as I lay in bed next to Laura, I couldn't sleep. I tried to make sense out of what had happened. I hadn't realized that when you try to do extraordinary things, you face problems that are equally extraordinary. You may think everything is going to be wonderful and carefree, but you quickly learn your new life isn't all cookies and milk. (I had been hanging around Laura and the kid too much.)

I recalled something my mother had told me years earlier: dreams have a way of becoming nightmares. Take one top-notch fantasy about a day in the park, add a homicidal maniac and before you know it you've got *The Silence of the Lambs*. Well, I was beginning to feel something like that was happening to me with the Miracle Weather. I should have been at the summit of my career. I had an opportunity only one other weatherman—the rain fanatic in Seattle—had been given . . . to actually control the weather. Yet, things were far from rosy. W.C. and Dexter were trying to run me out of the business. Edward was taking liberties with my forecasts, causing grief and confusion. Rev. Furrow had made me the target of his scorn. Laura was not very happy with me. And many Toledoans planned to do nasty things to me if they ran into me in a dark alley.

With a heavy heart, I realized the only thing that might make all of those people happy would be my fall from grace—and that was scheduled the next day.

Somehow, in all the hoopla and controversy surrounding the Miracle Weather, the real Jerry Sheldon had gotten lost. What could I do to get my life back on track? What could I do to salvage something of my livelihood and self-respect before the meteorological committee censured me and old man Bengolo threw me into the garbage can of life?

After hours of tossing and turning, I slipped on my shirt and slacks and drove over to the only place where a person can do serious thinking at four in the morning.

23

Scattered throughout Denny's restaurant were a dozen customers, a strange assortment of players in the comedy we call Life. A few seemed to be on their way home after late dates. Others, dressed in work clothes, appeared to be grabbing a quick breakfast before reporting to work. I suspected a few of the night owls were homeless souls trying to pass a few hours indoors, nursing a cup of coffee. And there was another group, those of us who couldn't sleep.

"I'd like to get my hands on the jerk who gave us this weather," growled the waitress. She was two inches shorter and a hundred pounds heavier than me.

I hunched down on the stool. "It's terrible. Just terrible," I agreed.

As I scrutinized the people around me, the wino on the next seat switched his empty cup of coffee for my full one and snatched my jelly roll. He thought I hadn't seen him do it. I was stunned at his audacity. I ordered another cup of coffee and sat it on my right side, out of the wino's reach.

"That's not a very friendly thing to do," the wino said.

I eyed him with disdain. "You've got a lot of gall. I paid for the jelly roll you snatched. It's mine."

"You're not big on sharing, are you?"

"Would you mind not bothering me?" I said crisply.

The wino headed off to the men's room. I sipped my coffee and pondered my predicament. I had been happy before Luther and I got so greedy. I had special forecasting powers that few people had ever enjoyed, Laura was willing to marry me, and national news coverage had made me something of a celebrity. People dream of making it big, and I had done it.

Then the dream turned sour. I became more and more greedy. Now, my job at WWTT was in jeopardy, and some of the biggest names in meteorology were coming to town to drum me out of the profession—my profession. The only thing I had ever wanted to do.

How could I put the pieces of my shattered life back together?

The sound of the wino's voice jerked me back to reality.

"Sometimes it helps if you talk about it," he said.

I glared at him. "Talk about what?"

"Something is bothering you."

I nodded. "Yes. You could say that."

"So what is it?"

"Look, I really don't want to tell you my troubles."

"Ah, go ahead, Jerry. I'm a good listener."

I was surprised the wino knew my name. I looked at him closely. He didn't look as though he owned a television, or sat around in the evenings watching the weather on WWTT.

"You've seen me on television?" I said.

"No. . . . Say, why don't you buy us a couple jelly rolls?"

"You've got a lot of gall."

"Aw, c'mon. Be a sport. Jelly rolls cost a lousy fifty cents. You can't spare that much?"

"Oh, what the hell." I signaled the waitress and asked for a couple jelly rolls.

"So if you haven't seen me on television, how did you know my name?"

The wino chuckled. "I know you pretty well, Jerry. ... *I'm Edward!*"

I nearly fell off my stool. I looked him over, from dirty brown hair to scoffed-up shoes. The closest he had ever been to Nieman Marcus had to be the trash bin in back of the store. He hadn't shaved in at least a week, and he smelled like a government-run nursing home. "You aren't Edward. How do you even know about Edward?"

He slipped a filthy arm around my shoulder. "I really am Edward. I saw you heading down here, and I figured I'd have a cup of coffee with you."

"But you're a bum. A wino!"

"You have trouble showing compassion for others, don't you, Jerry?"

"Yes. What can I say? That's the way things are today. . . . By the way, you could use a new tailor."

"So could you. . . . That's one of your problems, Jer. You're into materialistic things. You want to hang around with people who have nice clothes, fancy cars, money in the bank. You should look beyond appearances. Look at what really matters about a person. Or about life."

If Edward was trying to make me feel ashamed, he was doing a pretty good job of it.

"I suppose you're right. It wouldn't have killed you to take a bath, though."

"Yeah. I could have taken a bath, but I didn't. Big deal. I could have come to see you as a millionaire, but what would that prove? . . . So we are gonna talk about this superficial stuff all night, or you going to tell me what's on your mind?"

"What do you think is on my mind? My world is falling apart. Later today, some of the leading meteorologists in the country plan to drum me out of the profession. Forever."

"How did you manage that?"

"I had some help. Dexter and W.C. were jealous of my success. They've been forecasting the weather for thirty years and they still can't get the 24-hour forecast right."

I looked intently at Edward's face.

"What's wrong?" he asked. "Do I have jelly on my mouth?"

"No. I just thought of something. Are you an angel? Am I sitting here in Denny's having coffee and jelly rolls with an angel?"

"I'm working on it," Edward mumbled. "Someday I'll be an angel. The Boss says I'm like a student who bounces around college for twelve years and never graduates."

"When you read my forecast for Thursday, why did you say 'It's your funeral'? What's going to happen?"

"Did I say that? Hmmm. I don't remember saying that."

I sipped my coffee as another wino sat down on the other side of me.

"I'll tell you the truth, Edward. I wish I had never tried to control the weather. You do a much better job of it up in Heaven than I ever could."

The second wino looked at us wistfully, then moved to a table on the other side of the restaurant.

"It's not as simple as you thought, is it, Jerry? There's reason in the 'madness'. If the weather didn't change, people would go nuts from boredom. And the seasons are necessary for a purging, and a new beginning. And more than that, a lot of responsibility goes with the job. You hold lives in your hands when you control the weather."

"That's very profound, Edward."

"Right. To put it in simple terms—over-ambitious, over-confident, over-zealous, gung-ho weather forecasters should stick to reporting the weather and leave the big picture to me. Nothing personal."

Edward was pretty good when it came to twisting the knife after it was already in.

"I know. All the publicity and notoriety wasn't worth a dime when you get right down to it. . . . Do you want to know the truth? I was much happier when I was just a nobody forecasting the weather, flying off to hurricanes or floods and plotting revenge against old Hard Head McCullough. . . . It's been a wild two and a half weeks, Edward, but I know what I've got to do. After today, I'm returning control of Toledo's weather to you. Who knows how much more damage I would unleash on Toledo in another week and a half! From now on, I'll stick to being a simple weatherman. That is, if I can still find work in the profession."

Edward took a swig of his coffee. "Well, hang in there. It's not over till the fat angel sings. By the way, God gave me a message for you."

"A message for me?"

"Right. He said He expects to see you in church Sunday. Sure, old Furrow is something of a dullard, but you don't go to church for him. You go to worship the Lord!"

"Don't worry. I'll be there come hell or high water!"

"Don't use language like that! Now I've got to put a memo about it in your file. . . . Anyone have a pencil?"

Our waitress loaned him her pencil. He scribbled a reminder.

"A little advice, Jerry: Try not to get into any more trouble. Your record isn't too great—particularly after that run-in with Old Lady Bodecker."

"I know, I know."

"Well, I'd better be going." He got up and brushed dust off his jacket. "Don't take it hard. All things considered, you did rather well." He started off and then stopped. He must have thought I was looking at him like an abandoned kitten searching for a home. "I tell you what. You can still be a hero to Kathy. Tell her that a friend of yours said she's going to have a white Christmas—guaranteed! Three inches of snow on Christmas Eve, starting at 8:02 P.M. and ending Christmas Day at 6:30 A.M."

"That's some forecast!"

"When are you going to learn, Jerry? When you do it, it's a forecast. When I schedule it, it's a command performance."

"Right."

He put a hand on my shoulder. "Good luck, Jer. It's been fun. . . . Take care of the tip, will you?"

As Edward slipped out of the restaurant, I felt that a load had been lifted from my shoulders. I knew I had done the right thing by giving up control of Toledo's weather. Somehow, things would work out. Even if the committee censured me, I would persevere.

VI

In the Eye
of the Storm

24

The previous day's snowfall began melting as I drove to work Thursday. A few clouds were moving in. It was a seasonably correct day, tranquil and cool. I figured the Meteorological Society lynching committee would be impressed—if it could overlook the mounds of snow on the ground.

At the station, I stopped by the newsroom to exchange barbs with my colleagues.

Brent pointed to headlines in the *Blade* about the hearing that afternoon. "Let me ask you a hypothetical question: If someone who happened to work with you showed up at the hearing and testified against you, would you hold it against that person? Hypothetically speaking, of course."

I grimaced. "Hypothetically speaking, I'd announce during the next newscast that the hypothetical person has been going on steamy picnics in the park with a young woman who is not his wife."

Brent choked. "Of course, the hypothetical person would never say anything against his buddy who works at the station."

Pauley hurried over waving a fax. "Run for the lifeboats!" he barked. "This ship is sinking!"

"This ship is always sinking," Morty suggested, unperturbed.

"It's different this time," Pauley said, quivering with emotion. "J.P. says he's had enough. He's closing down the station!"

We were stunned. Brent took the fax from Pauley.

"You mean we're all out of jobs?" Fran asked.

"That's right!" Pauley exclaimed.

"Why didn't he just sell the station?" Brent wondered.

"He tried to. Couldn't find a buyer. He's going to shut us down and write us off on his taxes."

"Well, we knew it was coming," Harry grumbled. "The only question was when."

Pauley swallowed hard. "I know how you feel. The station has betrayed you. You're going to hit the phones, calling around about jobs, and I don't blame you. But we've got another week before we close up shop forever. Until then, I'd like you all to do your jobs like the professionals you are."

Harry patted Pauley on the back. "You're absolutely right, Pauley."

The rest of us nodded our agreement.

"Thanks," Pauley said, as he headed back to his office. "You're the best."

"I never thought Pauley cared," Morty said.

"Of course he cares," Brent said. "He's out of a job, too."

"I wonder if Reggie was fired," Fran mused.

Brent showed her the fax. "Reggie is J.P.'s new director of personnel. He sent the fax!"

"We're out of jobs and Reggie is climbing the corporate ladder," Morty lamented. "My world doesn't make sense any more."

"No offense," Harry grumbled, "but your world never did make much sense."

We laughed because we knew Harry was trying to make the best of a bad situation.

Disaster had befallen the station, but I had no time to reflect on the implications. It was time to head over to the SeaGate Convention Centre and face another disaster—my lynching at the hands of the Meteorological Society. My mood was dampened by the knowledge that even if—by some miracle—the committee sided with me, I was out of a job.

As I drove, I noted that more clouds were moving in from the southwest and breezes were growing stronger. I had not forecast rain, but it looked as though we were going to get some anyway.

The convention centre parking lot was full, and dozens of people had gathered outside the building. I had hoped only a few spectators would show up, but lynchings always did attract crowds.

Television news crews descended on me when I was thirty yards from the entrance.

"Jerry, some people are comparing this to the Salem witchcraft trials. How do you feel about that?"

"Did you know that ten thousand Toledoans signed petitions against you, Sheldon? How does that make you feel?"

"Where did you get that suit, Jerry—from the Salvation Army?"

I marched through the crowd and into the building.

About six hundred people already had taken seats inside the convention centre. A loud "boo!" erupted when I entered. A huge screen hung from the ceiling. The people in the back rows would be able to see everything very clearly.

Harry Delaney, my mouthpiece, sat glumly behind stacks of papers and law books. I pulled up a chair next to him.

"You were right," he said. "I shouldn't have taken your case. I need clients I believe in."

I gasped. "It's a little late to get cold feet, Harry!"

He shrugged. "Don't worry. I'm a professional and I'll give you the best possible representation. . . . Uh, would you mind paying me now?"

"Let's wait and see if I get out of this alive," I suggested.

"I was afraid you'd say that." He leaned over and whispered. "I want to be sure I understand this—you say it was the computer cooked by lightning that caused all this, and someone up in Heaven named Edward sends you the weather, but I can't use any of that in your defense."

"That's right."

"How do you feel about pleading insanity?"

"You know, Harry, I'm a little disappointed. I thought I was getting an attorney like Perry Mason, or Ben Matlock, or Percy Foreman. Someone who could get me out of this mess through sheer genius and hard work."

"Forget it. Houdini couldn't get you out of this mess."

A few minutes before 3 P.M. the Meteorological Society hit squad arrived. The four men and their woman colleague moved toward the platform like General Sherman marching through Georgia. I figured the woman was Miss Lanson. I recognized the others as some of the leading meteorologists in the country. The organization had sent its A-team.

More people piled into the arena and claimed seats. If this had been a City Council hearing, ten people would have shown up. But because it had to do with the weather—something everyone talks about—the crowds turned out.

Dexter Bentley and W.C. Muldoon occupied front row seats, grinning like school kids who had put tacks on the teacher's chair. Laura and Kathy sat in the second row.

In the rows behind them I could see Rev. Furrow, Hard Head McCullough, Luther Chambers, Beulah Morgan, Mrs. Bodecker, Eric Larkin and the salesman from the User Friendly Shop. It seemed like everyone who knew me was there, including three of my old instructors at the Toledo Weather College. Good grief. Couldn't they forget the mess I made of their classes and let bygones be bygones?

The committee's female member gaveled the inquisition to order.

"Good afternoon, ladies and gentlemen. I am Ruth Lanson of the National Meteorological Society." She introduced the co-conspirators who had traveled with her from Washington: Jeffrey Bacon, Horace Luginsky, Malcolm Whitelaw and Roger Olfinger.

"I'm sure you know why we are here this afternoon," she continued. "Two respected meteorologists in the Toledo area have made serious allegations about the causes of Toledo's recent unusual weather. Specifically, they believe Jerry Sheldon of WWTT has—through demonic or criminal means—sabotaged the weather in Toledo and by doing so has undermined the integrity of weather forecasters not only in Toledo but across the nation. This hearing is being held to determine if these allegations are true and, if so, to punish Mr. Sheldon. Both sides will state their cases and the public will have an opportunity to speak. Then, the five of us who represent the Meteorological Society will vote on the motion to censure Mr. Sheldon.

"Let us begin by hearing from Dexter Bentley, a legend in Toledo meteorological circles, who along with W.C. Muldoon filed the original complaint against Mr. Sheldon."

Dexter hiked up to the stage and faced the audience.

"Hello, friends and neighbors," he said. "As you know, I have been forecasting the weather in Toledo for forty-seven years. I have seen dramatic advances in forecasting technology during that time. I have seen major changes in the way weathermen work. But I have never seen anything like the fraud that this young upstart—this heretic—has perpetrated on Toledo. I could not stand by silently while this infidel destroys my profession and this wonderful city!"

Cheers and applause greeted Dexter's remarks.

"Exactly why do you feel Mr. Sheldon is responsible for Toledo's unseasonable weather?" asked Horace Luginsky.

Dexter glared at me. "Because he is a young, arrogant, irresponsible, low-down, conniving, drug-addicted, alcoholic low-life."

Miss Lanson sighed. "That's what you said over the phone. I was hoping for facts to back up your allegations."

"Yes, Dexter, how about some facts?" I said.

Dexter started pacing. "I'll give you facts," he snarled. "Number One, this all began after Sheldon and his weather computer were struck by lightning. Before that, our weather had been typically crummy for this time of year."

"Yeah!" "That's right!" "Crummy!" the crowd roared.

"Number Two, the next day Sheldon forecast it would be 82 degrees, though the rest of us called for a high of 28. The next day, the temperature reached 82 degrees. In December, yet!" He faced the panel straight-on. "There was no reason for it to be 82! It was completely unnatural. And yet there it was, and this snotty young upstart had forecast it!"

"That's right!" "In December!" shouted the crowd.

I couldn't let that go unchallenged. "So, Dexter, you want to drum me out of the meteorological profession because my forecast was on the money and yours was 54 degrees off the mark. Is that right?"

Dexter tore shreds of his hair out. "It had no business being 82 degrees! There was no reason for it! A weatherman couldn't predict weather like that unless he was possessed by evil influences! And it didn't happen just once. It went on day after day. He forecast crazy weather—and he was always right!"

"I wish I had this on tape," I said. "It would make great reading on my resumè."

Miss Lanson gaveled for other. "Mr. Sheldon, please refrain from interrupting. You will have your chance to speak. Continue, Mr. Bentley."

"Number Three!" Dexter boomed. "On at least two occasions, this young warlock forecast disasters specifically targeted at certain individuals—his retired neighbor and a fragile ninety-three-year-old woman in suburban Perrysburg."

"Fragile my foot," I snarled. "She could whip a wimp like you with one hand tied behind her back."

The crowd gasped as Miss Lanson gaveled for order.

"Nobody can target forecasts like that unless they are demonically possessed!" Dexter declared. "And finally, Number Four, this depraved individual has essentially admitted his guilt and responsibility for these acts by cashing in on them! He sold the movie rights for a million bucks! His agent is planning a line of Toledo Weatherman Frozen Dinners. And the stores are flooded with merchandise like this—"

He held up two items.

"—a Toledo Weatherman Doll and Toledo Weatherman Underwear!"

"Oh, for God's sake," Laura moaned, as she covered her face.

"With all this merchandising and promotion, he's making a mockery of our profession!"

"Wow!' said meteorologist Malcolm Whitelaw. I couldn't

tell if he was shocked or envious of my merchandising success.

"But Mr. Bentley. This is all circumstantial. Do you have any proof linking Mr. Sheldon to the weird weather?" asked Miss Lanson.

Dexter turned and confronted her. "I just gave you proof, you old biddy. What else do you need?"

Miss Lanson looked as though she had been slapped. "Mr. Bentley, you are out of line!"

As Dexter sat down and slumped in the chair, I heard rumblings of thunder. What had happened to the tranquil weather I forecast? Well, there wasn't time to worry about that now.

Miss Lanson primped her hair and tried to regain her composure. "Before we hear from Mr. Sheldon, is there anyone here who has anything to say?"

A clamor arose from the crowd. I told Delaney we might be there for two or three days.

"Doesn't bother me," he said. "I'm getting four hundred bucks an hour."

Anne Rubrick, manager of one of the largest malls in the city, took the floor. "This has been the most disastrous Christmas shopping season the merchants in Toledo have ever experienced. Sales are off forty-eight percent. Twenty of our stores that rely on Christmas sales are on the brink of closing down. The loss to Toledo will total several million dollars!"

"Nonsense," said Delaney. "What about all the tourist dollars that pumped up the city's economy?"

"The tourists came to Toledo to soak up the sun," Rubrick said. "They didn't come to shop. Sure, the tourism benefitted hotels, motels and restaurants for a while, but then it fell off and everyone has been hurting!"

"That's terrible," Delaney said sympathetically.

I glared at him. "You're supposed to be on my side."

Next up was Mary Lou Batchwalter, whose house was severely damaged by the same winds that knocked over WORY's tower. "This man"—she pointed at me—"is a public menace. He should be banned from the city forever. The winds he unleashed on Toledo made mincemeat out of my house. I had done nothing to him. I'm just a poor working girl. What am I supposed to do? Insurance won't cover the damage. I'm out six thousand dollars. And there are hundreds of other people like me. Jerry Sheldon's storms were responsible for millions of dollars worth of damage!"

"That's an exaggeration," Delaney objected.

Mary Lou pulled an envelope out of her purse. "Not at all! My attorney—who is filing a suit against Sheldon and WWTT—has prepared a list showing a preliminary damage total of two million, six hundred thousand, two hundred twenty-six dollars and fifteen cents."

"I had no idea it was so much," Delaney said. "By the way, you can add four hundred more to the total for the damage to my car!"

I leaned over to confer with my mouthpiece. "Harry, maybe I'm naive, but I thought since I was paying the bill, you worked for me!"

"I *am* working for you. I'm gaining their confidence by showing sympathy for their plight."

"How about being sympathetic to my plight?"

Delaney shrugged.

After several more Toledoans complained about storm damage and the committee received the petition against me signed by ten thousand residents, Beulah Morgan took the floor. "I could tell you about all the strange, weird and evil things Jerry Sheldon has done, but we'd be here for weeks!"

Delaney shrugged. "Go ahead. We've got time."

"Well, I don't," she snapped. "So let me just say that Sheldon has a lot of weird weather crap in his backyard, he threatened to dump a snowstorm on me, and he stays up late at night plotting what he's going to do with the weather. And I've seen strange people hanging around his house! I think they're messengers from the Devil!"

"That's ridiculous," I snarled. "What 'strange people' are you talking about?"

"There's one of them!" she roared, pointing at Eric.

Eric turned pale and slunk lower in his seat.

"That's Eric Larkin," I said. "He works with me. He's a cameraman at WWTT!"

"That don't mean he's not a messenger from the Devil!" Beulah declared.

The crowd gasped. Miss Lanson gaveled the meeting back to order.

Old Hard Head McCullough was up next. As he rose to his feet, his jaw jutted forward in defiance. His eyes were like cold steel. His words dripped with venom. "It has been my misfortune to live next to this miserable excuse for a weatherman for three years, and I can tell you that he's the worst troublemaker, the most conniving, lying, deceptive rascal, you could ever have for a neighbor. And I can tell you, too, that he's always doing very strange and mysterious things with the weather. As many of you know, one day he singled me out in his forecast—and two feet of snow fell on my property while everyone else's land was clear and warm. Now, if that doesn't prove he's into devil weather worship, I don't know what will. He's a menace!"

A commotion erupted again. Miss Lanson gaveled the meeting back to order.

Next up was Mrs. Bodecker, who made her way slowly

to the podium using a cane. She began speaking in a soft, gentle voice as befits an elderly lady, but it gradually grew louder and louder.

"I am Florence Bodecker and I live in Perrysburg. I am ninety-three years old."

I moaned, "Oh, for crying out loud. Everyone in the whole state knows how old you are. Let's move along!"

The committee was stunned. Mrs. Bodecker glared at me.

"You are a terrible person!" she grumbled. Then she faced the audience. "The only thing I ever did to this . . . this . . . imbecile was to send a beautiful quilt to him. It took me a month to finish it." She turned and looked at the committee. "Arthritis in my hands, you know." Then she faced me. "But in exchange for my generosity, this weatherman sent about a foot of snow my way the next day out of spite. Now, I don't know how he did it, but I do know that he is an *evil, evil person!*"

As Mrs. Bodecker uttered the last three words, she smacked the table where I was sitting with her cane.

"It was nothing personal!" I pointed out. "A weatherman shouldn't be forced to do remotes or acknowledge quilts that people send in!"

At that point, I don't think anyone—not even Laura or Kathy—was in my corner.

Miss Lanson glared at me. "Mr. Sheldon, a number of serious allegations have been made about your weather forecasting methods, and I must admit that Toledo's weather has been freakish recently."

"It certainly has!" I declared.

Delaney tried to quiet me so he could speak in my defense, but I wanted to state my own case. It was my turn to pace the room and seize the offensive. Wasn't it General

Patton who said, "Attack! Attack! Attack!" Maybe it was Donald Duck. I wasn't thinking very clearly, but I knew I must take the initiative.

"Toledo has had its share of unusual weather," I conceded, "but you know as well as I do that freakish weather occurs nearly every day somewhere in the country. The real question has been whether Toledo's weather professionals could meet the challenge when freakish weather like this comes our way. Would they run around like nervous nellies, conjuring up all sorts of wild stories?"—I glared at Dexter—"or would they keep their heads and do their jobs professionally? . . . Would they make up wild stories to compensate for their inability to do their jobs—like Dexter did—or would they call on all their resources and all their experience to deal with this unique situation?"

Dexter leaped toward me shouting, "Why you two-bit punk, I was warning people about blizzards and floods before you were born!"

Security guards restrained Dexter.

The lights in the convention centre flickered as a man in a tweed suit hurried up to the stage and handed Miss Lanson a message. After a few moments, she announced, "The cumulonimbus clouds that moved into the area have produced violent thunderstorms, and the Weather Service has just issued a tornado warning for the Toledo area. A tornado was sighted in nearby Ottawa Hills. I suggest we adjourn until the danger has passed in order that the local meteorologists in attendance can do their jobs, ensuring the public is informed about what is happening. The rest of us can take shelter in this building. We'll put television coverage of the situation on the big screen so everyone will know what is going on."

I motioned to Eric, who was sitting in the fifth row. "Let's go!" I shouted, as I hurried to an exit. "We've got a live one!"

25

We hurried through the parking lot and jumped into the WWTT van Eric had driven to the hearing. I drove so Eric would have his hands free to shoot film. I picked up the car radio and contacted Pauley. We put the warning on the air as I pressed the accelerator to the floor. It was a few minutes after 5 P.M.

"This isn't what you predicted," Eric said.

"It sure as hell isn't," I muttered.

I had wondered what had happened to the real me. Suddenly I knew. I was rushing off to be in the middle of the action, just like old times, and it felt good.

Heavy rain splattered the windshield, driven by thirty- or forty-mile-an-hour winds. The clouds overhead appeared dark and menacing. Thunder rumbled in the distance.

Eric and I raced to the northwest suburbs in the van, which was one of two WWTT vehicles equipped with production, engineering, recording and microwave transmission equipment—all of which Pauley had purchased second-hand, of course.

"I'll go out there with you, but if things get hairy, you're on your own," Eric said. "I renegotiated my contract with

Pauley last week. It says the station will not knowingly place me in a dangerous situation."

We sped west along Central Avenue.

"You're dumber than ox droppings," I said. "You've still got to do your job. All that clause does is relieve Pauley and the station of any responsibility if you get killed in action."

Eric gritted his teeth. "I'm tired of people takin' advantage of me. You mind pulling the van over while I buy a gun?"

I gulped. "Not now, Eric. We've got a weather emergency to cover."

By the time we reached Ottawa Hills, the winds had intensified. The two cellular phones in the van came in handy. Eric—who served as engineer as well as cameraman—communicated with Barb Farley over one of them as we prepared for live video transmission. Farley directed the operation from the WWTT offices. I listened to storm damage updates on a police radio and used the other cellular phone to keep Pauley posted on what was happening.

We scanned the skies, trying to catch a glimpse of a tornado. The eerie wall of dark clouds looked fearsome, but no funnel clouds were in sight.

"Maybe we lucked out," Eric suggested.

To the west, a patch of sky appeared even darker than the clouds around it. Within seconds, I could tell it was a twister. And it was headed our way.

"Get us on the air!" I barked into my phone as I tried to keep the van on the road.

Eric began shooting video.

"Stand by!" Farley said.

Eric focused on the twister as it danced menacingly in our direction, lifting up telephone poles like toothpicks and tearing rooftops off houses. I thought of something Peter Felknor had written in his book *The Tri-State Tornado*: "All through my childhood we seemed to be on the run from these storms." As the sky darkened and rain poured from the heavens, I described the scene:

"TAKE COVER! OTTAWA HILLS AND THE TOLEDO AREA ARE IN THE PATH OF A TORNADO WHICH HAS THE POTENTIAL TO DO A LOT OF DAMAGE. THE WINDS IN THIS TWISTER PACK A LOT OF POWER. POLICE REPORT IT HAS ALREADY RIPPED THROUGH THREE HOUSES AND—OH, NO!—IT JUST SLAMMED INTO BOWLING HORIZONS!"

Bowling Horizons was one of my favorite hangouts.

"BOWLING BALLS ARE FALLING OUT OF THE SKY LIKE DANDRUFF OFF BRENT LASSITER'S SPORT COAT."

Eric said, "Let's get out of here!"

For once I agreed with him. We were crossing the line from risk-taking into foolish abandon. I turned sharply to the left and gunned the accelerator—only to see another twister coming at us. I slammed on the brakes. Terrifyingly strong wind blasts blew the microwave antenna equipment off the van. We couldn't send back live shots any longer, but we'd have some great footage to air later if we lived through the confrontation with the twisters.

Over the phone, Pauley pleaded, "What's going on? Come in, Jerry. Are you there?"

"Affirmative," I said. "We're in the path of two twisters. They've ripped up at least a half dozen homes and a bowling alley. We're heading out of here."

"Just remember, Jerry. That van is company property. You lose it, you pay for it."

"You can stop being a company man, Pauley. J.P. is shutting down the station. Remember?"

"Oh, right. Well, try not to damage it too badly."

There was no hope for Pauley.

The twisters drew closer. A few minutes earlier I had felt relatively safe. Now two funnel clouds were in the neighborhood.

Through the monstrous rain, I could see an elementary school a half block up the street. The parking lot was filled with cars! As we drew closer, we could see a sign: "SCHOOL PLAY TONIGHT".

I turned to Eric. "Shall we bail out and sacrifice the van?"

"It works for me," Eric said.

"Jerry? Eric? What's going on? Speak to me!"

Those are the last words I heard from Pauley before Eric grabbed the camera and I grabbed both of the cell phones and we jumped out of the van. We dashed to the schoolhouse as rain drenched us and winds pelted us with debris.

"I've gotta get a better job," Eric grumbled. "What are we going to do, Jerry? We're sitting ducks."

"Yeah. Kind of reminds me of Miami."

"I'm gonna kill you," he muttered.

We hurried inside the school. Hundreds of people were crowded into the school auditorium. Eric caught the storm action on video, shooting through a window in the school lobby. Using my cell phone, I described for viewers what was happening. Rain was still coming down hard. The winds were ferocious.

Suddenly, I realized one of the twisters was bearing down on the school. My weather was completely out of control. In a minute, the school could suffer a direct hit. Who knew how many people would die!

I shoved my cell phone at Eric. "You describe what's happening!"

I talked to Pauley on the other phone. "We've got big trouble! Just do what I say! Talk to me on the phone in my weather room."

"Why? . . . Have you been drinking, Sheldon?"

"Just do it!"

Ten seconds later, he picked up the phone in my weather cubbyhole.

"All right," I said. "On my weather computer keyboard, type this message: 'Attention, Edward! It's an emergency! Help!'"

"Who's Edward?" Pauley asked. "Is he on the payroll?"

"Just do it—fast!"

"All right, keep your shirt on."

I waited breathlessly.

"Nothing happened," Pauley said. "What now?"

"Type the same message again. He's got to be there!"

The tornado blasted through a house only two blocks from the school. Wooden beams sailed through the air like toothpicks.

"All right!" Pauley said. "Edward says he's there."

"Type this: 'Tornado nearing school. Many will die. Stop it!'"

"All right," Pauley said.

A few tense seconds later, I demanded, "Well? What did Edward say?"

"Nothing," Pauley replied.

"Keep repeating the message!"

I had done everything I could do. I grabbed the other phone away from Eric.

"THE TORNADO IS A BLOCK AWAY, MOVING RELENTLESSLY CLOSER," I said. "IF IT HITS THE SCHOOL WE'LL HAVE A MAJOR DISASTER ON OUR HANDS. HUNDREDS OF PEOPLE ARE HUDDLED IN THE SCHOOL AUDITORIUM. . . . THE TORNADO'S A HALF BLOCK AWAY NOW. IT JUST

SLAMMED INTO A VAN, PICKING IT UP AND HURLING IT FORTY YARDS DOWN THE STREET!" I was breathing heavily and sweating profusely. "THE TORNADO IS ALMOST ON TOP OF US! WE ARE OUT OF TIME!"

"WE'RE ALL GONNA DIE!" Eric shouted.

I feared he was right. My heart raced as I mumbled a prayer. So this is how my life will end, I thought. Pulverized by tornadoes I created. I closed my eyes for a moment or two, fearing the worst.

When I opened my eyes, I was amazed.

"SOMETHING STRANGE IS HAPPENING," I reported. "THE TORNADO HAS STOPPED DEAD IN ITS TRACKS. . . . NOW IT'S FOLDING BACK UP INTO THE CLOUDS. THE WINDS ARE DECREASING . . . BOTH TORNADOES ARE GONE! THE SCHOOL WAS NOT HIT! . . . AND NOW THE CLOUDS ARE SHRINKING AND MOVING OUT!"

A minute later, sunlight filled the sky.

I continued to report over the cell phone, describing the tornadoes and the damage they had wrought and interviewing people who had been inside the school, while Harry Vincent sped out to Ottawa Hills with our other van. We were on the air with live video from Ottawa Hills again in time for our 6 P.M. local newcast. By then the scope of the damage was clear. Eight homes had been destroyed, several others damaged. Bowling Horizons and a laundry were totalled. No one was killed, but an elderly couple suffered minor injuries.

I finally understood why Edward had said "it's your funeral" after I placed my order for a mild day with clouds. I should have realized that with warm and cold fronts clashing and clouds moving in, conditions were ripe for tornadoes. And *I* was responsible for the injuries and the property damage. If it hadn't been for Edward's timely intervention, there would have been many more injuries and deaths. He had said the fate of many people was in my hands. Now I knew what he meant.

After the newcast ended, Harry drove Eric and me back to downtown Toledo. I spoke with Pauley on my cell phone. "Everything is under control," I assured him.

"Was our van totalled?"

"You could say that. The pieces are spread over three counties. If it's any consolation, it died a valiant death. Forget about the van. You did good, Pauley. And tell Edward he saved a lot of lives."

"Who *is* Edward? I don't understand any of this."

"I'll explain it to you some other time. Right now, an angry mob is waiting to burn me at the stake."

26

"Drop me off at the convention centre," I told Harry. "A few hundred people aren't done humiliating me."

Eric sighed. "What's the matter with them, anyway? I didn't see Dexter and W.C. out there risking their lives to tell people what was going on."

"Different strokes for different folks," I muttered.

I climbed out of the van and Eric headed back to the station to edit the film for the late newscast.

I considered passing on by the convention centre and just walking until I ran out of road, but I could see headlines about the "chicken weatherman" and decided to face the music. Besides, everyone else had their say. Now, I could finish my defense of my actions before they lynched me.

I entered the convention centre and started down the center aisle toward the stage. Someone in the back rows shouted, "Hey, it's Jerry!" and a few people started applauding. Then more people applauded. The next thing I knew, nearly everyone in the place was standing up and applauding. I couldn't figure out what was going on. Maybe they had voted to kick me out of the profession and were giving me a final send-off. When I reached the stage, the meteorological committee stood.

"Don't I get to finish my defense?" I asked.

"No need for that," asserted Roger Olfinger. "Everyone here saw what happened on the big screen. You were right in the middle of the action, reporting what was happening, trying to save lives. We don't know what happened to Toledo's weather over the last two weeks. Maybe you had something to do with it, maybe you didn't. But whatever went on here wasn't demonic. Perhaps all the people in Toledo have been part of something special, and it was fortunate that you were here to help people understand what was going on."

"Besides," Jeffrey Bacon said, "anyone who was facing a hearing to determine his fate would be crazy to schedule tornadoes the day of the hearing."

Dexter jumped out of his seat. "He *is* crazy! He's responsible for this whole mess—the heat wave, the snowstorm, the rain, the tornadoes—all of it! He did it all!"

I shook my head. "Dexter, poor Dexter. You've been handling Toledo's weather too long. You need a long rest."

Dexter's face flushed. His blood pressure must have been sky high. "Why you snot-nosed punk. You've been screwing around with the weather for two weeks. Now, you think you can duck responsibility by pretending you had nothing to do with it. Well, it won't work! Admit it! You have seized control of Toledo's weather!" He turned to the committee members. "If you don't believe me, ask W.C.! He'll tell you."

W.C. seemed to be weighing the pros and cons. I was no longer a goat, I was a hero. W.C. would look ridiculous if he attacked me as Dexter was doing. "I think Dexter is mistaken. The Weather Service office in Toledo was on top of this from the start. Dexter obviously misread some of the weather maps, and—"

"What?" Dexter bellowed. "You old turncoat! You agreed with me! You said we'd get Sheldon if it was the last thing we did!"

"Why, Dexter," W.C. responded, sounding like the Voice of Reason. "The Weather Service wouldn't treat a fellow weatherman like that."

"Well, I think we've heard enough," Miss Lanson declared. "I see no reason to prolong this. It's clear we were mistaken, and we owe a debt of gratitude to Jerry Sheldon."

Dexter's eyes glazed over. "But—you've got to believe me. Sheldon did it. Somehow, he got control of the atmosphere over Toledo and he's making a mess of it! He didn't save lives—he nearly killed us all. He's got to be stopped!"

Miss Lanson stood. "We apologize, Mr. Sheldon. Mr. Bentley apparently has been under quite a strain. He obviously snapped."

"Such a shame," W.C. muttered.

"But I'm telling you the truth!" Dexter boomed. "Am I the only one who can see what's going on here?"

Two security guards took Dexter by the arms and escorted him off the premises. He was a crushed man.

Miss Lanson said, "We will draft a statement for the news media commending you for your tornado coverage tonight and condemning Mr. Bentley for wasting our time. Now, if the kind people of Toledo will excuse us, we have a plane to catch."

Well-wishers eagerly shook my hand. Laura kissed me as Kathy looked on. I told Laura I had given control of the weather back to Edward. "From now on, I won't be able to create the weather. I'll just forecast it."

Kathy sighed. "I was hoping you would make sure we had a white Christmas."

She looked so serious—and so disappointed.

"Well, I heard from a very reliable source—I mean *a very reliable source*—that, as a special present for you, snow will begin falling on Christmas Eve at 8:02 P.M. and end Christmas morning at 7:30. Three inches of snow. You will have your white Christmas."

Anger flashed in Laura's eyes. "Jerry, you just said you weren't going to mess with the weather anymore!"

"I didn't! I'm just reporting what I was told. Edward said to tell Kathy she'll have a white Christmas."

Kathy's eyes opened wide. "He really said that?"

"He sure did, honey."

Kathy pondered the new development. "You know, I think I want to be a weather forecaster when I grow up."

"Try stealing cars or robbing banks," Laura suggested. She turned to me. "I'm proud of you, Jerry."

"You are? A week ago you talked about breaking off our engagement."

"Yes, but I knew you would do the right thing."

I stared at her dumbfoundedly. "Why have you been giving me such a hard time if you knew I'd do the right thing?"

"Someone had to tell you what the right thing was."

At the edge of the crowd of well-wishers, a man in an exquisitely tailored suit that must have cost two thousand dollars waved, trying to get my attention. It was Edward! He pointed to something a few feet away—a glowing figure. It looked like an angel . . . a rather plump angel . . . and she was singing.

27

The WWTT newsroom was a madhouse that evening as our small staff mapped out details of our tornado coverage. It was a big news story, and we felt confident we had better coverage than the competition. As the video was edited, I wrote and fine-tuned the script. Brent seemed to be spending a lot of time on the phone. I figured he was trying to line up another job.

Shortly before the 11 P.M. newscast, Pauley trotted out of his office waving another fax.

"Gather round, boys and girls!" he shouted. "There's been a change in plans! The station isn't being shut down. J.P. found a buyer after all!"

We were stunned.

"Who bought the station?" asked Harry.

"J.P. didn't say."

Pauley sat on Brent's desk.

"The new owner might be worse than J.P.!" Fran suggested.

That thought boggled the mind.

After a few moments, Brent piped up. "Would you mind removing your ugly butt from my desk, Pauley?"

"What? Oh." Pauley stood up.

"That's one of the things you're not allowed to do. Not now. Not ever."

We stared at Brent. He was acting stranger than usual.

"There are going to be some changes around here," Brent said.

"What are you talking about?" I asked.

"I bought the station."

"What?" the rest of us said in unison. It was the first thing we had ever done together.

"I'm too old to look for another position," he said. "I wanted some job security. I bought the station with money I had saved over the years. Now there won't be any more memos from New York telling us when to crap. There won't be any more ultimatums from you, Pauley, telling us to suck up to the bigshots."

"I'll start packing," Pauley muttered, as he started back to his office.

"Not so fast!" Brent grumbled. "I will continue to anchor the news. That's what I do best. And I want it clearly understood that from now on, your job is to run the newsroom but you don't order me around. You can make suggestions, and I'll consider them."

"You mean you want me to keep my job?"

"Yes, but stay out of my hair. And, Pauley—we're not going to do Happy Talk. If we've got something to say to each other, it won't be because some idiot consultant told us to! Understood!"

"Sure, Brent. I mean . . . boss."

Brent smiled. "Things are going to be much better now. The way I see it, the biggest problem I've got is Sheldon."

"Me?"

"That's right. You and I don't always get along very well,

but your new contract with Pauley is almost unbreakable. And when I looked at your salary, I couldn't believe it! You make more than I do!"

"I have a good agent," I said.

"Uh-huh. In any case, I don't like it when you make fun of me. I don't like it when you tell people the weather is the important part of the newscast—the news is just filler. What am I going to do with you?"

"I'll try to stay out of your hair, too, Brent—what little there is of it."

"That's what I mean. Do you suppose you could be nicer to me?"

"I don't know, Brent. You make such an easy target."

"I could cut your weather segment down to thirty seconds."

"Maybe I could be nicer to you, Brent."

"Good idea."

Pauley collapsed into a chair. "I need a vacation. A very long vacation."

The weather headed the newscast, of course. Eric's video appeared on the monitor as Brent led into my report . . .

"Two devastating tornadoes ripped through Ottawa Hills this evening, leaving behind a trail of destruction and more than a million dollars in damage. Two people were injured. Jerry Sheldon has the story ..."

I took the cue. "The scene in this western Toledo suburb was one of devastation and despair. Out of the west and north came savage tornadoes which ravaged eight homes, a bowling alley and a laundry."

Through my earphones, I could hear Pauley in the Control Room …

"Don't forget our van!"

"… AND A WWTT MOBILE VAN. MIRACULOUSLY, A SCHOOL IN THE PATH OF A TORNADO WAS SPARED AT THE LAST MOMENT WHEN BOTH TORNADOES DISAPPEARED AS QUICKLY AS THEY HAD COME. HUNDREDS OF PEOPLE WERE INSIDE THE OTTAWA HILLS ELEMENTARY SCHOOL WATCHING A PLAY AT THE TIME."

After the commercial break, we ran footage from the Meteorological Society hearing. Brent commented …

". . . AND THE COMMITTEE HAILED JERRY SHELDON FOR HIS COVERAGE DURING TODAY'S DEVASTATING TORNADOES. SHELDON'S COLLEAGUES AT WWTT KNEW ALL ALONG THAT HE WOULD BE EXONERATED. YOU CAN CONTINUE TO WATCH SHELDON'S FORECASTS EVERY WEEKNIGHT ON WWTT—AND EVERY WEEKEND, TOO, UNTIL WE FIND A NEW WEEKEND WEATHERMAN.

"I AM ALSO PLEASED TO ANNOUNCE TONIGHT THAT WWTT HAS BEEN SOLD. THE NEW OWNER—THAT'S ME—HAS ISSUED ASSURANCES THAT WWTT WILL CONTINUE TO BRING YOU THE FINEST IN NEWS, SPORTS, NETWORK PROGRAMMING AND, OH, YES, WEATHER."

VII

CLEANING UP

28

Harry Vincent agreed to handle the weather chores over the Christmas holidays so I could be with Laura and Kathy.

On Christmas Eve, I drove Laura and Kathy over to the Fourth Baptist Church to hear Rev. Furrow's holiday sermon. On the way home, Kathy searched the skies for signs that it would snow later that evening.

"What happened to Luther?" Kathy asked. "Is he still your agent?"

"Afraid not," I said, as I turned off the interstate. "When he found out I didn't have control of the weather anymore, he dropped me like a hot potato. He's trying to sign up a kid down in Alabama who claims he can turn stones into gold."

Kathy thought that over. A few minutes later, she said, "Do you know what might be cute? … Little toy weather computers named Edward. Push a button and they squirt rain on you. Push another button, and they pelt you with snow. I'd buy one of them."

My heart raced. Toy weather computers! They could make a fortune! I thought about calling Luther back and telling him to get the deal in the works. Then I noticed Laura glaring at me and the urge passed.

We drove by Dexter Bentley's two-story brick house on the west side of the city. I was stunned to see heavy snow falling on Dexter's property. It hadn't started snowing anywhere else—only on his yard.

"Jerry!" Laura snapped. "You promised you wouldn't do that anymore!"

"I didn't. This one was all Edward's."

Dexter, bundled in an overcoat, shoveled mightily as we drove by, but he wasn't making much progress. Snow was piling up fast.

"Hi, Dexter!" I shouted. *"Nice weather, isn't it!"*

Apparently he didn't think so. He hurled the snow shovel in the direction of my Buick as we drove by.

We arrived home shortly after 7:30 P.M. I opened the drapes on the large picture window in Laura's living room and the three of us gazed at the sky. It was overcast, but no snow was falling. Kathy was not worried.

"It's not time yet," she explained. "Edward said it would start at two minutes after eight."

Laura sighed. "Kathy, something like this would be very hard to arrange. Don't be disappointed if it doesn't snow on time."

Kathy looked at Laura very sternly. "Edward wouldn't tell me something that wasn't true."

I had a sinking feeling that perhaps Edward had gotten busy with taking a nap, or choir practice, or something like that, and had forgotten. It would break Kathy's heart.

And then—at precisely two minutes after eight—fluffy flakes of snow began fluttering to the ground. Edward had remembered.

Laura noticed I seemed apprehensive.

"Why are you worried?" she asked. "It's just like Edward said! It's beautiful!"

"Yes, but you don't know Edward. We could get five or six feet of this stuff before he remembers to turn it off. He's like a forgetful old man who leaves the water running in the bathtub. Now, when I was in charge of the weather—"

"When you were in charge, nobody could figure out what was going on—including you!" Laura reminded me.

That took the wind out of my sails.

Laura and I were married three days later. I moved my things into Laura's house. Eventually, we will look for a larger house. Laura wasn't very happy when I set up my weather equipment in the backyard, but I explained that it was necessary for my work. I said it was a package deal. If she took me, she had to take the equipment too. In one of her pettier moments, she asked if she could keep the equipment and get rid of me.

I have adjusted to my new surroundings, more or less. And just so I don't miss the old neighborhood, old Hard Head McCullough comes over every once in a while to sabotage my rain gauge in the backyard.

I finally got a new weather computer. The old Cloudchaser is in my study. I can't forecast the weather on it anymore, but sometimes I converse with Edward to see how he's doing. And every so often, just to annoy Dexter Bentley, Edward gives me a little inside information on storms headed our way.

FORGET ABOUT TV QUIZ SHOWS— THIS IS THE BIG TIME!

A NEW CAT IN THE HOUSE CAN CAUSE A LOT OF TROUBLE AT CHRISTMAS

A tale of two cats during the Christmas season. It's for readers of all ages.

Smokey and Boomer

JACK GILHOOLY

FOR AVAILABILITY SEE AMAZON.COM

NOTABLE NONFICTION
FINE FICTION
AND COOL HUMOR

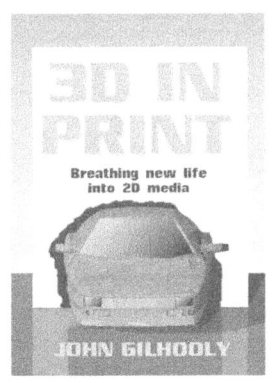

FOR AVAILABILITY SEE AMAZON.COM

www.ingramcontent.com/pod-product-compliance
Lightning Source LLC
Chambersburg PA
CBHW072051170626
46813CB00004B/1299